I0602106

That's My Story

A novel

Steven Key Meyers

That's My Story

Copyright © 2021, 2022, 2024 Steven Key Meyers
All Rights Reserved

ISBN: 978-1-7368333-9-1 Third Edition
Published by Steven Key Meyers/The Smash-and-Grab Press

No part of this publication may be reproduced, stored in a retrieval system or transmitted in any form or by any means, electronic, mechanical, recording or otherwise, without the prior written permission of the author.

The characters and events in this book are fictitious, except for historical characters and events treated fictionally. Any similarity to real persons, living or dead, is coincidental and not intended by the author.

Part I, *The Last Posse,* was first published in 2018.

SMASH
&GRABpress

Also by Steven Key Meyers

Fiction
The Holy Hugs of Father S.

My Hollywood Memoir and Other Fiction
(with *Sidestep, Big Luck* and *Save The Max Man!*)

Family Romance

My Mad Russian: Three Tales
(with *Another's Fool* and *I Remember Caramoor*)

Queer's Progress

The Wedding on Big Bone Hill
(with *Junkie, Indiana*)

Springtime in Siena
(with *The Man Who Owned New York*)

All That Money

Good People

Nonfiction
The Man in the Balloon:
Harvey Joiner's Wondrous 1877

Plays and Adaptations
A Journal of the Plague Year,
and Other Plays and Adaptations

The Midhurst Lashes
A screenplay adapted from A.C. Swinburne's novels

I. The Last Posse

for my Uncle Bing,

George Lentton Meyers, Jr.
1917-2011

At 12 you know as much as you ever will — or more, since at that age you're still in a state of nature and can cleave through to the heart of the matter.

— Jean Stafford
The Catherine Wheel

1.

WE SIPPED OUR COFFEE as the sun stabbed its first flat rays into the town. Uncle Jim liked to take the pot up to the roof, said it was the only peace he got. Made it himself on the kitchen stove, next to the swill Aunt Wilhelmina—her my classmates called *the terrifying shemale*—was boiling for the prisoners.

Looking out between crenellations of the jail's castle roofline we could see everything. Vernon, Texas was a metropolis of 10,000 in those days; it's shrunk some since. The courthouse across the street—three stories tall—was brick, as were our two-story Sheriff's Department with lock-up and living quarters, both banks, the Wilbarger Hotel and the Methodist-Episcopal Church. Every other establishment on the public square was wooden and had a gabled false front. Wooden houses with front porches and gable roofs crowded up behind the square on all four sides.

The rising sun sharpened the gables into arrowhead shadows and launched them in slow motion.

Uncle Jim said it amused him how that solemn march of shadows imprinted steeple shapes on the town.

"Don't believe it," he said. "Behind their fronts, people here're like people anywhere. Not so bad, really, but take 'em at face value at your own peril." In 1922 Jim Groves, still shy of 40, had been Sheriff of Wilbarger County for 15 years.

I lifted my big cup (about half milk) and looked out over the parapet with—judging from the smile he cracked—his own solemn expression.

From below we could hear wagon wheels turning, horses nickering, Model Ts sputtering, voices raised in greeting; could smell fresh manure and oily automotive exhaust, and see the wind biting at the cornucopia of coal smoke blowing skywards from the approaching 7:48. The morning clouds were still novel to me: coconut macaroons pressed against glass, pink on their eastern sides.

Uncle Jim was talking about the big day we had ahead of us: A famous bank robber named Frank Holloway was being handed over to his care to await trial. Exactly one year earlier Holloway had robbed (allegedly) the bank in Harrold, a hamlet to the southeast. November's the time to do it—the cattlemen sell out and deposit their take, the farmers, too. The robber had sidled indoors, revolver in each hand, politely ordered the safe opened and bags filled, and left with $12,000. That was a *lot* of money in those days.

Uncle Jim said from the moment the call came in he suspected Frank Holloway. He was famous thereabouts—*the Oklahoma Yeggman,* they called him.

"What's a *yeggman?*" I asked. Didn't know of any in California, where I come from.

"Safe-cracker," Uncle Jim told me. "Newfangled word for an old-fashioned thing. Just another outlaw." Classic black hat, he said, silver-plated Colt .45 on either hip—each with seven notches, one for every man he'd killed—silver spurs and high-heeled boots.

Uncle Jim had rushed off to Harrold to investigate, even as Frank Holloway was getting back to Vernon and standing drinks at the Wilbarger Hotel, Prohibition be damned.

Then he vanished.

"You know him?" I asked.

"Oh, for years. As Sheriff you have to meet a lot of characters you really wouldn't rather."

I was flattered, taking this as said for my possible distant benefit. Uncle Jim had three sons—Shorty, almost a year older than I, Otha, 15, and Ted, 16—who seemed too football-crazy to go into their father's line; at the moment, they were off at Terrill Prep in Dallas building a boarding-school football dynasty.

"What's he like, Frank Holloway?"

"Snake. *And* a bit long in the tooth to be doing what he does," said Uncle Jim. He looked at me. "That means old."

"He's *old?*"

"Not so very—my age, thereabouts. But hair going thin, gut getting thick, some rust in the joints. Too old to be robbing banks. That's a young man's game. Like being Sheriff. Should be talking about what a hotshot he used to be, 'stead of trying to be one still." He smiled. "Like me."

Said it was mortifying to know whom he was looking for but finding him plumb gone. Timing the bank robbery with the railway schedule, the yeggman boarded a fast train north, Gladstone bag in hand—whisked away before Uncle Jim realized it. Since then, nothing.

Nothing, until a few days earlier, when word came from the Texas Rangers in Austin. The Chicago Police Department had telephoned. Seems they'd arrested a man for pickpocketing in Grant Park, were about to send him down for a stretch in Joliet when he started spinning yarns, claiming to be Frank Holloway, the Oklahoma Yeggman wanted for a litany of crimes. Took credit for that big British Columbia job a few months back— $350,000!—and also the one in Harrold, Texas.

Not that they believed him, they told the Rangers, but thought they should call. Didn't believe him because their pickpocket looked like a bum.

Here the Rangers brought Chicago up short: Good, yes, they'd made Holloway for that Harrold robbery, could they please come get him?

Uncle Jim said that was doubtless Frank Holloway's whole idea—escape the clutches of Chicago P.D. and get to Texas, where he'd recant his confession and insist on a jury trial. Bank robbery? If convicted, five or ten years in prison, but with a jury who ever knows what will happen? So it was a shrewd play. Anyway, today the Rangers were handing him over, from now on he'd be Uncle Jim's headache, his guest in the calaboose downstairs.

He pulled his long, booted legs off an embrasure and planted his feet flat, signaling he had something serious to say.

"Bad stuff, Frank Holloway. Has a hooligan sneer that rejects *me, you, Vernon,* any stab at decency. Feels entitled to take whatever he wants. Undercuts the rest of us just trying to get along and do the best we can. That yeggman's bad stuff."

As he drained his cup, I begged him not to make me go to school that day, and without fuss he agreed. I was stunned—son of schoolteachers, I knew school was sacred—but his mind was on his yeggman.

"Hungry, Bing?"

"You bet, Uncle Jim."

"Let's get out of this hoosegow, go find us some chow."

2.

I WAS WHAT they used to call a pretty boy.

Not good.

"Precious!" the biddies would go. *"Adorable!* Features like a *doll!* If only my Mary had those *curls!* And his *complexion* — peaches and *cream!"* What really got them? My freckled button nose: *"Awww!"*

Other boys? Don't ask. But it toughened me up, be sure of that. Classmates never made kissy sounds at me, not after the first time. Learned early how to fight, and though I was never big, I was pretty good. My Texas sojourn helped me grow out of being pretty, though years later Ben Johnson, my movie-star neighbor in Pawhuska, Oklahoma told me I could have tried my luck in Hollywood.

At my prettiest when I turned 12 years old and my parents sent me and my rosy-cheeked blush, ringlets framing wide-set blue eyes over an upturned nose, off to stay with Uncle Jim and Aunt Willie. I was a raving beauty! On Labor Day when I was expecting to start school in Pasadena the following week, Dad put me on the train for Texas — Ma said goodbye at home, she was feeling poorly — and I ended up entering 7th grade in Vernon.

Hadn't met Uncle Jim before, but knew he was Ma's favorite brother. He called her his baby sister. I'd heard the stories, also about how big the Groveses were in Vernon. The four brothers lived in town, as did Gram and her widowed daughter Effie one block behind the square, in a wooden house with a front porch and a gable roof. Gram—*very* old, over *70!*—was the tiniest woman I ever met. A shrimp myself, not five feet tall, I towered over her. Bent over, wearing long dresses and bonnets tied under her chin, she looked tough as a fairy-tale witch. Well, Ma said she had to be tough to raise a family on a ranch in the middle of nowhere and have her husband die on her in the prime of life while she was expecting their seventh child.

Gram looked me up and down and said sourly, "My, ain't you a pretty thing."

The Oklahoma Yeggman was due on the 9:17. From the roof we went downstairs, past the apartment where Aunt Willie was washing dishes, to the jail on the ground floor. Six freshly-fed prisoners looked out at us like something didn't agree with them. Didn't say anything, though. However bad the food, they soon learned that complaining was a mistake. It didn't change anything and was resented—not so much by Uncle Jim as by Aunt Willie.

The deal was that the County paid her, as official jail cook, 25¢ a day per prisoner, and anything she didn't spend on meat or eggs or butter and the rest she could keep.

Well, she managed to keep most of it. Knew every trick in the book, so the prisoners got watered-down porridge, soup with sorry scraps afloat in it, watery stews, liquefied sauerkraut, jellied ham, mashed potatoes that found their own level in the bowls she served them up in.

Jail's not a holiday camp, she'd tell them, *nor a dude ranch neither. Learn what jail is, won't be back.* So howevermuch she pocketed, she claimed to be saving the County money in the long run. Anyway, her kitchen. Uncle Jim left it to her, except for making his own coffee, spooning in the grounds and an egg and letting it boil.

In the office he just checked to see if his deputy wanted to go eat, too. His deputy was his enormous, melancholy brother Reuben.

Uncle Rube was hungry sure enough, so leaving Aunt Willie to hold the fort — she was assistant jailer, too — we three tramped up the sidewalk, careful not to step on the crack Shorty's head made when he fell out the window as a baby.

The Swasteeka Restaurant occupied half the ground floor of the Wilbarger Hotel. The hotel boasted 20 rooms, but Uncle Jim said it wasn't a very good one — he'd seen better in Fort Worth. I liked it, though. Downstairs was all polished wood, bronze gaslight fixtures and shiny brass railings. Before Prohibition the restaurant was a saloon, where in 1895 the sheriff of the day was shot to death trying to break up a fight. The floor still had bloodstains. There was always a warm buzz of conversation from the leading lights of town joshing one another while they ate.

Everyone greeted Uncle Jim and Rube, was greeted in return. Our table beside the window ruled the room.

We sat down and were served our eggs sunny side up, bacon, sausage, grits, biscuits and gravy, more coffee, and Rube nodded outdoors. I knew the story that was coming; he told it every few days. Always on his mind, apparently.

"That's where your Ma and Jim and me saw them hang the reverend," he said.

Uncle Jim's predecessor did it, and it remained Vernon's sole legal public hanging, for the predecessor never cared to repeat the experience, nor had Uncle Jim any hankering to be a hangman. The reverend had poisoned his wife with strychnine and gone off with the choir's soprano, but not far enough.

When he was condemned — despite appeals from his lawyer, Sam Houston's own son — the Sheriff volunteered to do the honors himself. From miles around people crowded into the square to witness the once-in-a-lifetime event, and they trooped the pupils over from school.

"Make room for the children!" the Sheriff bellowed from the gallows, next to him the reverend looking as if his mind was already on other things. "Let the little children up!"

I knew that Ma, then just 9, never could get the sights nor sounds out of her mind, though Rube said she closed her eyes tight at the drop.

"All right, Rube," Uncle Jim said.

"Uncle Jim," I asked, "how'd you get to be Sheriff, anyway?"

"Well, old Sheriff Ish was a friend of Daddy's, like a father to us after he passed, and when he saw me getting big and strong, brought me in as deputy. So when he retired, I took over."

"Oh!"

He sighed. "Always wanted to be a cattleman, but that's all right. But when you're Sheriff, sure better know which way the wind's blowing."

Rube nodded solemnly.

"Now, then: Frank Holloway. We'll go over, meet the train. He'll be cuffed to one or both of the Rangers, and they might want to hand him over on the spot, but we'll ask 'em to bring him to the jailhouse.

"Take Holloway's belt, empty his pockets, put him in an end cell, keep the next one vacant. Rube, you disarm and go in the cell with them, help uncuff him while I hold a gun and Bing holds the door. Bing, let the Rangers and Rube out, and lock him up. Got it?"

"Sure, Jim."

"Got it, Uncle Jim."

"He's a slippery S.O.B. Don't like having him here. This afternoon for the hearing — *arraignment* — Rube'll cuff him up in his cell — I'll hold the gun and you, Bing, the door — and take him

14

over. Bring him back the same way, stuff him in 'til trial, 'less he bonds out, though I don't expect he will. Trial should be next week."

"OK."

"Just have to be careful." Uncle Jim shoved a forkful of egg into his mouth and licked yolk off his mustache. "Bing, ever get the chance, take a look at the famous photograph of Six-Shot Stan finally being hauled in to Fort Smith, Arkansas. Stands there grinning like an idiot, deputies on either side, sheriff in front, but four seconds after the flash powder goes off, the lawmen are dead and he's running.

"Well, look close, and while the sheriff's standing *proud* in front of the camera, highlight of his *life,* you can see that despite the cuffs Six-Shot's already got his hands at his gunbelt. Gun comes up *blazing.*"

"What happened to him, Uncle Jim?"

He patted his lips dry.

"Didn't get far. But I don't intend on being that foolish. Hey, how'ra *you,* ol' Bossie?"

Said this to the man I already knew was Mayor, chatted with him about getting that yeggman, big day for our burg, and so forth.

Then the Mayor's eyes narrowed and he nodded at the far wall.

"Jim, don't know what those two Slicks are peddling," he said, low. "Brooklyn Bridge, for all I know. But they wear perfume."

"Look into it," Uncle Jim assured him.

The Mayor went on his way. I turned around and looked. The Slicks were from out of town. Hell, they were from New York! One was the father, other his son. They'd rolled into town a week earlier, taken the suite upstairs, been getting to know people. I'd noticed them in the back of the ME church on Sunday, putting their heads together and seeming to assess members of the congregation. When we Groveses emptied out of our pew and went up the aisle, one nudged the other.

They made it their business to get to know my cousins Harry Groves and Ginger Groves. Harry was 20, Ginger 19 — family in town closest to my age, so I hung around with them. That's how I knew what the Slicks were "peddling," and it was even more exciting than the Oklahoma Yeggman!

But I didn't volunteer anything. No one had to tell me to keep quiet, even before Harry and Ginger spit-swore me to silence; instinctively I sensed my uncles' knowing about it might make it go *poof!* like a dream.

Now Uncle Jim gave the Slicks a hard look. Didn't faze 'em. The younger smiled back like he was having fun.

But they were for another time. Uncle Jim looked across at the courthouse clock and said, "We better git."

3.

MY FIRST SATURDAY in Vernon, Uncle Jim drove me out in his official Model T to visit his father's grave in the cemetery rising over Beaver Creek 20 miles south of town. A sister was buried there, too.

He had to squeeze behind the wheel — six foot three, 230 pounds, all of it muscle. Never felt smaller in my life than sitting next to my Uncle Jim. Biggest of four big brothers, he was the son of an even bigger father.

That grandfather of mine, Nathan Micajah Groves, was legendary to me. Came of poor but good Southern stock, Uncle Jim said, brought to Texas as a boy, and at 13, big for his age, fought Civil War battles in a Texas militia, even getting to Sand Creek, and after that hunted buffalo and homesteaded two different places, ending up with the Beaver Creek spread, and blacksmithing in addition. Gram showed me her tintype of him, and it was startling, even scary, to peer into it and meet the incendiary eyes — onyx eyes *afire* — of the wild man staring back, hair and beard long and black. My grandfather.

From a long ways off we could see the graveyard's cottonwood trees. Not many other trees around; Uncle Jim said they got thinned out whenever hard times hit and people had to cut wood to survive. A wrought-iron railing protected a few dozen graves in various stages of neglect. My grandfather's stone was the biggest, a white marble slab four feet tall carved with his name and dates and symbols my uncle said were Masonic; big Mason, his dad. Next to his grave was his little girl's—Nelly, dead at 2 years old by the same typhoid fever that took him. Her marker was a stone carved in the shape of a pillow.

It was a boon to the family when, in the 1890s, the Waggoners started acquiring land along Beaver Creek. They paid top dollar, made it possible for my grandmother to buy a house in town and for Ma to go to school and enjoy an easier life than the ranch ever afforded.

Ma was 7 when Gram sold out, and though her stories would make you think the ranch was a showplace, when Uncle Jim took me out there that day all I saw were the silvery remains of a few barns and fences near a dugout house. The land, never tilled, had a funny feel to it, too, as if the big-bluestem and Indian grasses were swaying at the top of the world, where the air's thin, the possibilities stark. The Waggoner Ranch now encompassed the horizon in three directions.

"How Dad loved it out here," Uncle Jim said softly. "Wild, in those days. Used to see buffalo, wolves, even panthers.

"And the sandstorms! Remember your Ma was raising a little calf she loved dearly when a sandstorm drove a piece of straw—*straw!*—through its throat, and it bled to death in her arms."

I was glad to get back to town.

Everyone said of all the sons, Uncle Jim most resembled his father, but he seemed anything but wild; instead, about as sad and gentle as Uncle Rube.

Now we walked over to meet the 9:17. Vernon was planning to build a brick railroad depot with ladies' and gentlemen's waiting rooms, a café, toilets, baggage rooms, crew quarters, stone columns out front and a platform under glass; I'd seen the pictures. But for now the Fort Worth & Denver City Railroad station was a shack beside an open platform.

We stood among those waiting for the train to Amarillo. The September day of my arrival, I'd never felt heat of the intensity that enveloped me when I stepped off in Vernon. Windows open across the endless Panhandle—flattest place on Earth—it was just bearable, but I stepped into a furnace. For all that the sun was setting, heat radiated around me as in an oven just turned off. A breeze came up, so searing I wished it would stop.

"How's your Ma?" Uncle Jim asked first thing, and I said, "Fine." But he always wanted to hear about her, her house and garden, her work as principal of the girls school.

Today, in November, it was better, the sun angling in low and vegetation going brown. Around us stood livery stables and garages, grain warehouses, a cotton gin, overhead a water tower painted *VERNON* in flowery script. We could see the backs of houses, with their lean-tos and outhouses and chicken coops, dogs big and small patrolling the alleyways. High on a wall across the street was a billboard of cowboys, Indians and bucking broncs painted in garish yellows and reds: *Pawnee Bill's Historic Wild West Show June 21, 22.* For two Junes ago. *That* was the Texas I craved, more like Ma's stories than this colorless agricultural town.

Finally—but right on time—the train steamed in under ballooning clouds of smoke, the panting engine a naked monster of pipes and exposed works, the coupling-rods *jerking-jerking, slowing-slowing,* with a gush of steam *stopping-stopping.* The engineer snapped off a salute to us.

We strolled down a few cars and stood aside as ranchers and farmers in coveralls got on and off. Last off were two Rangers in white Stetsons, one attached at the wrist to a man faded and insignificant as an ageing farm hand.

"Sheriff Groves?" a Ranger called, and Uncle Jim stepped forward to shake hands. "Got your omelet for you."

"Your yeggman," clarified the other.

"Good, good. Yeah, that's him. How you doin', Frank?"

"Hey, Jim. Better when I've had my bath and shave and manicure and—"

"Don't mind, gentlemen, show you to the jail, just this way."

The Rangers came right along.

All the time Frank Holloway's pinched dark eyes shifted back and forth as he looked for a way out, tapping at the walls (figuratively) for a spot that would give.

"This is it, fellas: *Vernon, Texas,*" he spat. "One-horse town, I said? Try one *pony.* Shit, Jim: *Chicago?*"

"Nephew, Frank. Watch the language."

"Sorry. Sorry, kid."

Now his eyes settled on *me.* Sized me up head to toe, like he knew a shameful secret and was going to spill. My skin prickled as I realized how deceptive that home-boy appearance was: The eyes he looked out of were cut-outs in the walls of Hell! Gave me the heebie-jeebies. No wonder he was a lousy pickpocket—get too close, your skin crawled.

"Say, but ain't you a pretty thing! *My, my,* make somebody a good wife someday."

For *me,* that did it, far as Frank Holloway was concerned.

Frankly, what a disappointment. My first famous outlaw was short, had bags under his eyes, hair matted where he'd slept on it, raggedy clothes—baggy dungarees soiled at seat and knees, torn shirt, stained jacket. *Stank!* And when did he last trim that gray mustache?

Meanwhile Jim chatted with the Rangers. How was the trip? Had breakfast? Time for lunch before the train back, maybe see the sights? Oh, too bad, the famous Red River crossing at Doan's is worth seeing. Next time for sure.

Walking through the courthouse square we created a stir. People stopped in their tracks, and some jeered. They knew

Frank Holloway.

"Not looking so sharp today, Frank!"

"That your convict outfit, Frank?"

He ignored them, as did we, and we jogged up the two steps into the Sheriff's station, office to the left, staircase straight ahead, cells to the right.

It went as Uncle Jim had laid it out, he holding a gun while Rube and the Rangers took the prisoner's belt, emptied his pockets, brought him into a cell.

As instructed, I shut the door behind them and watched closely. They removed his handcuffs and, while Frank Holloway sat down on the bunk rubbing his wrists and pushing out his lips in annoyance, I opened the door to let Rube and the Rangers out, quick clanged it shut again, and we had him. I was relieved: I didn't like this Oklahoma Yeggman, not one little bit.

He spoke up. "One thing, Jim: No disrespect to Mrs. Groves, but can you please ask the hotel to send in my meals?"

"All right," said Uncle Jim. Not his way to coddle prisoners, but who could blame the yeggman? And while Frank Holloway was paying for food from outside, Aunt Willie got to keep the whole County meal allowance.

After he signed their papers, Uncle Jim had me take the Rangers back to the station and wait for their train with them.

"So this is Vernon," one announced like he didn't think much of it.

"Yes, sir."

My face caught his eye. Doing the grand survey of blush, lashes, curls and nose, he started to say something. Then, bless him, stifled it.

"Here we go, Charlie," he murmured instead, as a locomotive hysterically worked the curve into town.

4.

I WAS AFRAID Uncle Jim would send me on to school, but instead he took me with him to see the court clerk.

We avoided the courthouse's grand stone staircase by entering through the ground-floor city marshal's door flanked by green globe lamps. City marshals were the town police force, and Uncle Jim said hello to everybody as we went on through and upstairs.

The clerk was delighted, said Judge Ohlmacher would be, too, and arranged the hearing for 2:00 o'clock. He wondered aloud if, after he was convicted, the yeggman might not cough up some bank loot in exchange for a more lenient sentence.

Then we stepped into the Swasteeka to arrange for Frank Holloway's meals. They were happy, too.

"Hasn't any money," Uncle Jim warned. "Pauper, for all I know."

"Oh, Mr. Holloway's credit's good with us, Sheriff. And we know his tastes — big beef man. Harvey'll take his food over." The proprietor nodded at his skinny delivery boy.

"Fine," said Uncle Jim. So that was settled.

But he caught sight of the Slicks sitting at the same table where they'd had breakfast. Lounging between them was my cousin Harry, son of Uncle Jim's and Rube's brother Eustace. Uncle Eustace was the local Willys-Knight dealer, and Harry worked for him. I liked Harry. He'd graduated from high school two years earlier and vowed that he was getting out of Vernon, didn't know *how*, didn't know *when*, but he was *out* of here soon as he had enough money saved!

Slicks leaning into him from either side, he sat against the wall looking flattered. I knew they were trying to get those savings out of him. Harry had $500 in the bank and, as it happened, that was exactly the sum the Slicks said they needed to start wresting our fabulous New York inheritance out of the wrong hands. I hoped he'd pay it over soon.

Planning what to do with *my* share of that colossal estate was keeping me up nights. Quivering with excitement, I lay awake for hours spending and investing my millions, building mansions for everybody I liked, founding schools and orphanages, buying jewels and dresses for Ma, books and candy and cars for myself. Did I want a yacht?

Riches on the scale I was anticipating, I found, bring their own problems. Meanwhile Aunt Willie remarked that I was looking pale and beleaguered in the mornings, and wondered what I was getting up to at night.

Now Uncle Jim walked across the Swasteeka, boots thundering on the floorboards. I tagged along.

That tramp of doom made the Slicks rear back. Standing up, Harry put a big smile on it, hurriedly shook hands with them, and walked out calling, "Hi, Uncle Jim, hi, kid. Later."

The Slicks got up, smiled, put out their hands.

"Sheriff, been wanting to meet you," said the elder. "Your nephew's told us about you and your distinguished family. Foster Bueche! My son, Foster Bueche, Junior!"

He pronounced it *Boosh*.

Uncle Jim shook their hands, said nothing as he sniffed their cologne.

They were a sight. They wore blue woolen suits with silk

vests, the elder's with a gold chain draped across it, and were freshly shaven and trimmed from Dawdy's Barber Shop across the lobby. The younger, maybe 20 years old, was handsome, with blue eyes and curly hair of a reddish cast. His father's voice had a lilt new to me—now I know it was an Irish brogue. He looked like his son, but in a flushed and overdone version. Uncle Jim said later the Sen-Sen on his breath told you everything you needed to know: He was a drinker.

My uncle starting to sit down, the father quickly said, "Take a seat, do take a seat." I took one, too.

"Time I welcomed you to Vernon, gentlemen," said Uncle Jim.

"Why, thank you, Sheriff, appreciate that. Texas hospitality's something, ain't it? Everyone's being so nice."

"Mr. Bueche, perhaps you'll enlighten me as to what you and your son are doing here?"

"Of course, of course." Leaning, Mr. Bueche reached to his feet. Looking under the table, I saw his hand go into a leather case. Bringing his closed fingers up to the tabletop, he opened them, and there was someone's *teeth*. I *jumped*.

"We're in *dentures,* Sheriff." His bright look drilled deep into my Uncle Jim. "Seen your Doc Weaver, later on we meet Doc Sheffield. Represent a factory in New York City—Lower East Side of Manhattan—worked by the most delicate-fingered Chinese ladies you ever saw! When a dentist makes a mold and ships it to us, we sculpt, color and polish a set of the finest dentures money can buy."

Uncle Jim's eyes drilled right back. "That right?" he asked.

I looked again at the ivory grinning from hinged pink gums.

"Doing business in the way of the future," Mr. Bueche said. "Till now, dentist like your fine Doc Weaver had to make his own dentures, with results painful all around. Can't expect one man to excel at extraction *and* bridgework, can you?"

"What else?" demanded Uncle Jim.

Would he tell him? For several nights running, when supposedly I was having supper at Uncle Eustace's or Uncle Clois's, in fact I'd been right there at the Swasteeka eating steak and hearing the Bueches explain the Groves Claim and its ramifications to Harry and Ginger.

Mr. Bueche, staring deep into Uncle Jim's eyes, decided.

"Well, Sheriff, there *is* something else," he announced, getting to his feet. His son stood up also. "Come upstairs, away from prying eyes, and we'll lay it out for you."

"We're all right here," said Uncle Jim.

Exchanging looks, the Bueches sat down again.

"Came to Vernon to sell dentures, Sheriff, but when we got here and discovered your family – the *Groves* family – I realized we know something you might not: That you and yours are the missing heirs to the Groves Claim!"

5.

"GROVES CLAIM? The Hell's that?"

Mr. Bueche produced a cigar. "Sheriff?"

"No thanks."

Bringing out a little scissors, he cut off the cigar ends and sloppily, wetly shaped them—all the while studying Uncle Jim without looking at him.

"Junior, why don't you go upstairs and fetch the documents?" he affably asked his son. "We'll risk exposing them to the public eye."

"Yes, sir," said Foster Junior. He got up and left.

More lipsmacking before Senior struck a match and started sucking at his stogie. I thought its aroma wonderful, but liked his cologne even better. Reminded me of Ma.

Signaling for coffee, he offered it all around. I would have accepted except that Uncle Jim didn't move a muscle.

Coffee brought, Mr. Bueche asked for cream and sugar, and the waitress apologized, said she didn't know where her mind was today, she well knew his tastes in the matter.

"All right, Sheriff, let me explain," said Foster, Senior. "The Groves Claim concerns a farm your ancestors used to own—used to own and, by rights, their heirs-at-law *still* own it."

He blew smoke, smacking his lips and gazing steadily at Uncle Jim. I thrilled: Until now, the Claim had been a secret — intangible, improbable, even somehow *dirty*. Sprung into the light of day, it suddenly assumed realistic contours. Could feel the money in my hand!

"The chain of ownership begins with one Nathan Micajah Groves. Unusual name, but the same as your father's, am I not correct? Well, this gentleman was a storied privateer of the Seven Years War. Know what a privateer is?"

A shake of the head.

"'Course you know what a *pirate* is? Privateer's same thing but *legal* — legal and *respectable* — commissioned by government as part of its navy. Nathan Micajah Groves came of Tidewater Virginians who sent their sons to sea: There was money to be made in transporting tobacco, slaves and so forth. Groveses were sea captains for generations, and made a good thing of it, too.

"During the Seven Years War — French and Indian War, some call it — Nathan Micajah Groves offered his services to the Crown and enjoyed signal success, capturing two — some sources say *three* — French ships of the line, for which King George gave him fabulous rewards: The sum of £10,000 is mentioned — $50,000 *then*, twice that today."

He was speaking to persuade.

"Unfortunately, one well-aimed cannonball closed Captain Groves's career. Spared his life but took off his leg — left leg at the knee. But recuperating in New York, he had the good fortune to fall in love with a local farmer's daughter, Amelia Edwards, and married her.

"The happy newlyweds retiring, rich and respected (those always go together, don't they?) to his ancestral Tidewater, they bought a plantation and cultivated tobacco. No more voyages for Cap'n Groves!"

At this juncture, Foster, Junior returned carrying a leather portfolio under his arm.

"Now, we've not worked out every link of descent. Must be done, of course, but to set the scholars to poring over old records takes time and frankly *money*. But I think your father most likely was the privateer's great-great-grandson."

Nothing from Uncle Jim.

"Amelia Edwards' family farm comprised 120 acres. Tell me if I'm mistaken, but that's hardly of a size to impress *Texans?*"

Uncle Jim held his own counsel while Foster, Junior informed us that the Waggoner Ranch exceeded *one million acres.*

"But did I mention that Amelia Edwards was an only child?" his father asked. "Heiress to the whole little place? And its location, you ask? That's what's so special, sir: Lower Manhattan Island, running from Wall Street almost to Canal Street, its western limit being the Hudson River, its eastern boundary Broadway."

Leaning back, eyes locked on my uncle's, he softly intoned, "Yes, sir: The most valuable 120 acres in the *world*. On them stand the *Woolworth* Building, the *Singer* Building, office towers, apartment blocks, tenement houses, factories, warehouses, stores without number. My son and I have penetrated to the sub-basement of the New York County Courthouse and there with our own eyes inspected tax rolls showing the total assessed value of the Edwards farm today—the Groves Claim—to be *one billion dollars.*"

After letting this figure resound for a few moments, his son murmured, "A little less, to be exact: Assessed last year in aggregate at 961 *million,* 744 *thousand,* 300 and 23 dollars."

For all that I'd heard it before, I was *electrified.*

"A *huge* fortune, Sheriff Groves," said his father, "and it's *yours.*"

I trembled, trying to grasp just how much money that was. Doing a lot of that lately. It meant that Uncle Jim, his brothers, sisters and their children, all the good privateer's descendants—

me — were richer than Rockefeller! My nocturnal castle-building had left me feeling guilty and bleary-eyed in the mornings, but now that Uncle Jim knew all, I could revel in it and exult.

A long silence. Uncle Jim said, *"And?"*

"That's it, of course," sighed Mr. Bueche, leaning back deflated. "You've hit on it, sir: There's a squatter — illegal *squatter* — on your land, a greedy and retentive entity called Trinity Church.

"How it gained possession of the Edwards farm is the crux of the matter.

"Trinity Church stands on Broadway at Wall Street, and the Edwards family were congregants. On the eve of the Revolutionary War, Amelia Edwards Groves' parents, fearful of British occupation of New York, removed themselves to their son-in-law's Virginia home. But first, to secure their property in their absence as best they might, as well as to benefit their beloved parish, they executed an instrument transferring the farm and its harvests to Trinity Church for ten years."

Mr. Bueche sighed, which his son took as his cue to open the portfolio and carefully take out oversized pages which he laid on the table away from the coffee cups. I could make out old-fashioned handwriting that looked strangely flat, like a printed book. That flatness Mr. Bueche explained by saying that these were *photostatic reproductions* of original documents kept *under guard* in the Grand Street vaults of the Bank of New York.

"You see there, Sheriff, a copy of the document of transfer, specifying the ten-year term."

But Uncle Jim continued to stare at Mr. Bueche. I couldn't read his expression.

"Clear and forthright. First, see the signatures" — Mr. Bueche's finger hovered — "and the date of execution — April 19, *1776* — and the date on which this instrument was to lapse, the farm reverting to possession of the Edwards family: April 19,

1786. With me thus far?"

Uncle Jim could have been Comanche, he was so impassive.

Mr. Bueche went on regardless.

"Well, in 1786 when Amelia Edwards Groves's mother returned to New York — her husband having died in Virginia — intending to move back into her house and plant her crops, she found the house demolished and her fields sprouting buildings, and Trinity Church disclaiming any knowledge of her or of their agreement — flatly refusing to return her property. Having no heart for lawyers, the old lady went back to her daughter's and soon enough died.

"Later, tobacco having exhausted their soil, Nathan Micajah Groves's sons began moving south and west in that diaspora that is the very chronicle of American history, some descendants ending up in Vernon, Texas." He nodded respectfully. "Seems in fact that other branches may have died out, leaving your Vernon one as sole Claimant. This must be ascertained, although, frankly, the Claim's so very large it hardly matters should cousins heretofore unknown emerge in whatever numbers.

"To prise the Edwards Estate — the *Groves Claim* — out of the clutches of Trinity Church at this late date must be done as a matter of justice," he sternly informed Uncle Jim, "but it will require a lawsuit, and lawyers cost money.

"Now, you ask how we happen to know these things, my son and I? Well, my own great-great-grandmother was first cousin to old Mr. Edwards. We're *cousins*, Sheriff — four times removed, I make it? Five times to the boy?" He beamed at me. "But I hasten to assure you that we assert no interest in the Claim, though not objecting should our new-found relatives" — his eyes sparkled — "prove generous."

I looked at my uncle through the golden tissues so deftly woven in front of my eyes, the filter through which I viewed most everything lately, and it jarred: He was there and not there. My *Uncle Jim* had vanished. Who remained was someone unknown, implacable, hostile and hard.

"Mr. Bueche, please put your papers away," he said, "and I suggest you take your son and your *teeth* and be on your way. It's not flattering to be taken for a mark, but if you're off today I'll try to overlook it."

Bueche's son looked pained. "But— But— But—" he sputtered. His father put a hand on his arm.

"Of course, Sheriff. Sorry to have offended. If you'll permit us to keep our 3:00 o'clock appointment with Doc Sheffield, your dentally suffering townsmen will thank you, and then we'll seek out a good train east—"

"Dad, we paid in advance for tonight!"

" —unless by generous forbearance you permit us to stay one final night?"

"Mr. Bueche, if you're here past noon tomorrow, my wife will be only too happy to extend her hospitality to both of you at the jail."

"Thank you, Sheriff. She's too kind."

6.

WALKING BACK to the jailhouse, I was mighty upset: Did this mean I wasn't going to be a millionaire?

"Uncle Jim, don't you *want* to be rich?"

He looked at me with surprise.

"*Rich?* Take us for suckers, Bing: They can say that land belongs to us, but it doesn't, nor is it theirs to give. Have that story and those papers—whatever *they* are—but they want something, and two guesses *what*. Think you'll find the first step to claiming your so-called inheritance involves paying over a lot of cold hard cash. And that's the whole point: Find enough suckers, they won't have to hawk dentures any more."

"But—"

"Bueche is a confidence trickster, Bing. Nothing more. Money doesn't grow on trees—*ever*."

"No one's saying it grows on *trees,* Uncle Jim," I rejoindered in frustration. "It's in the *ground.*"

Thought he'd understand: There was oil around Vernon, and people were getting rich just by owning the land over it.

He looked at me, registering my tone.

"Only surprise, Bing, is they're not trying to sell us the Brooklyn Bridge, like the Mayor said. Least that exists. This story of theirs? *Fantasy.* A *lie.* Think we wouldn't know about it if it were true?"

32

Well, but— Well, but— No, how *could* I know that?

As we went into the jail, the Swasteeka's Harvey was just coming out, looking dazed and honored to have personally delivered the Oklahoma Yeggman his luncheon T-bone!

Rube said everything was quiet. Most days the brothers had lunch at the hotel, but today Uncle Jim wanted to hang close— just in case—so we ate Aunt Willie's ham sandwiches. Not bad, either: She was in a good mood, the yeggman representing the best of both worlds, no food to fix *and* a meal allowance.

After eating, I went to see my cousin Harry to tell him about Uncle Jim's throwing the Slicks out of town. Found my way to Uncle Eustace's Willys-Knight dealership, Vernon's fanciest building, brick with stone accents, plate-glass windows showing off the shiny red model inside. Others were parked under the porte-cochère or out back, by the three-bay garage.

Harry did OK selling cars for his dad—the Willys-Knight was a rakish roadster, not only fast but tough; Model Ts could scoot with impunity anywhere you aimed them, but so could the Willys-Knight, and in considerably better style.

Found Harry in the showroom, smoking morosely, one foot on the model's bumper. It was a beauty with a gold pinstripe.

"Hey, kid." Turned out he'd bought the Slicks lunch, so knew all about their set-to with Uncle Jim.

"Uncle Jim says those Slicks're making us their marks!"

"Jim don't know *squat*. Jesus Christ, Bing, it's a *fortune* just lying there waiting for us to pick it up! Ask any businessman, have to *spend* money to *make* money. Jim's an all-right sheriff, but a businessman he *ain't*."

"Aunt Willie is."

"True."

"What'll we *do*, Harry?"

"Take it easy, Bing, we're on it, Ginger and me." Then he changed instantly. A man in coveralls who had driven a muddy

Model T slantwise up against the showroom now entered. Harry trod on his cigarette, straightened up and was smiling all over even as he pushed me firmly towards the garage.

There I watched them tighten belts and clean carburetors for a while, before trailing back to the jailhouse to help chain up the yeggman for his hearing.

Frank Holloway still looked like a gone-to-seed country boy as we escorted him across the square. People told him so, too, jeering at his chain-clanking baby steps. But, eyes flashing hellfire, apparently he could care less.

My first inkling that things might not go according to plan came as Uncle Jim and Rube hustled him into the courthouse through the marshal's office and behind us I heard a smooth, powerful engine. Turning, I saw a yellow Pierce-Arrow— *gorgeous!*—round the square and park in front of the courthouse. A man and woman got out and traipsed up the steps.

The hearing was supposed to be routine, binding Frank Holloway over for trial and letting him enter a plea. I'd already seen several arraignments in the dusty courtroom beneath the late Judge Handy's distinctly squiffy portrait. After 40 years on the bench, Judge Ohlmacher always got us out in record time. Long white hair moving in time with his gavel, he radiated a nimbus of power surprising in a district judge.

His clerk convened the hearing, the judge entered, the driver of that Pierce-Arrow introduced himself as Dennis Love, attorney-at-law from Wichita Falls and the prisoner's counsel. Judge Ohlmacher asked the prisoner if he understood the bank-robbery charge against him—"Yes, Your Honor"—and how he wished to plead: "Not guilty, Your Honor."

"Understand you confessed in Chicago?"

"Beat it out of me, Your Honor. *Not* guilty."

Judge Ohlmacher scheduled the trial for the following Tuesday and set bond, with a malicious smile drawling, "Bond of $12,000" — naming, of course, the sum the yeggman withdrew (allegedly) from the First Bank of Harrold.

"Yes, Your Honor," said his lawyer. "Post that right now, if you please."

Sensation!

Mr. Love approached the clerk's table and placed on it a paper-wrapped package. Muted greens caught the light as the clerk tore it open and crisply counted bills. Someone had predicted the bond's exact amount. Frank Holloway smirked.

"Unchain the prisoner, Sheriff," said the judge. "Mr. Holloway, you are free to go until Tuesday morning, when I expect to see you in this courtroom at 10:00 a.m. *sharp.*"

"Thank you, Judge."

There was quite a commotion at this turn of events. Several depositors of the Harrold bank had crowded into the courtroom to gawk at the Oklahoma Yeggman, and were aghast at the sight of *their* money being paid over to secure his freedom.

Uncle Jim and Rube unchained Frank Holloway where he stood, left him rubbing his wrists and ankles and whispering to his lawyer and the lady who accompanied him. Who she was, I never knew.

What our yeggman did next, as a free man, I know only by report, for Uncle Jim and Rube marched me back to the jail: He strolled across to the hotel and, finding its only suite already engaged, took the second-best room and sent word to Dawdy's Barber Shop that he required immediate tonsorial assistance, including a manicurist, and also notified the haberdashers — *Craig & Son Gentlemen's Outfitters* — that their attendance was required. A bottle, too, was procured.

The upshot was that several hours later, as sunset cast steepled shadows that reversed dawn's, Frank Holloway was strolling at his ease around the public square, elegantly turned out in a new black suit, smooth-shaven, hair trimmed and pomaded, mustache black as night, the unknown lady of the Pierce-Arrow hanging from his elbow as he went along shaking hands. I watched from the jailhouse roof, stretching my head out through the embrasures except when he turned my way, when I drew back lest he see me. No one razzed him now that he was free and looked dangerous.

But I saw what the yeggman was doing in parading his spiffed-up front around town: *playacting*. Frank Holloway, I sensed, didn't actually belong anyplace, and he knew it, so had to pretend he owned everything in sight, and for whatever reason people bought it. That mask of his was all there was to him; he lived in other peoples' sight. What did that make him, a reflection? Not really anyone at all!

I knew about playacting myself. My parents being reassigned every year or two, I'd already attended four schools in three neighborhoods, so had mastered the fine art of fitting in; a matter mainly of *pretending* to fit in. In effect I was two people, the pretty little boy on view and, behind that mask, myself; a self still in formation and not yet to be revealed, but decidedly *not* pretty! I considered myself way more dangerous than Frank Holloway.

Uncle Jim came up to the roof and found me.

"How it goes sometimes," he said quietly. "Bad guy gets away with it. But let him strut, don't bother me none. Tuesday morning he's on trial, and no way he's not going down. Five years at Hollingsworth Penitentiary, the old slave plantation? See him strut about *that!*"

7.

AS SHE ASSURED the County Commissioners every year when she bid for the jail contract, Aunt Willie ate what she fed the prisoners. "Eat same as them," she'd declare. "Plain home cooking." Judging from her sourpuss, she didn't like it any better than they, but eat it she did.

So Uncle Jim and I went off for supper at the Swasteeka as usual.

Crossing the lobby's Brussels carpet to the dining room, we could see that the Slicks were there with my cousin Ginger. The elder Bueche gave Uncle Jim a nod expressive of sorrow and disappointment. But Junior and Ginger were too caught up in conversation to notice us. Seemed to take a kick under the table to make Ginger startle, slide up the wall and hurry out the door. For all that he was considered slow, Ginger, after apprenticing with East View Cemetery's gravedigger, had lately leased a steam excavator from Uncle Eustace and started his own business digging out foundations and laying pipe for the County; he was prospering.

We turned to our regular table by the window, and Frank Holloway grinned up at us from it, a bright, aromatic confection of pomade and cologne, silver buttons and gleaming hair. Next to him sat his woman and his lawyer.

"Why, Sheriff!" he called. "Come on ahead, sit yourselves

down, plenty of room. No, no, no, no, no, no, no — *insist!*" Uncle Jim had swung away, but saw that it was the only table with empty places. "I don't bite!"

Chompers on view, though, it looked like he might. Ma would have sniffed at his charm campaign as typical of a man *all hat and no cattle.*

Working knife and fork on a tremendous sirloin, Frank Holloway turned out to be quite the talker.

"Know what you're thinking, Sheriff. When I paid over that $12,000, you thought I was paying with the fruits of that same robbery you're putting me on trial for. But why would I keep loot lying around for a year when a man's got to live, and live well? *Hmm?*

"No, bond money came from the Royal Bank of Victoria, British Columbia. Cracked the safe there six months ago."

"Telling me straight out?" Uncle Jim demanded.

Frank Holloway chewed and swallowed. I could feel the hellfire heat behind his eyes. He was scary.

"What're you going to do about it, *extradite* me? Doubt it. Told 'em in Chicago, and they didn't bat an eyelash. Guess I'm home free with that one — $50,000, my share. Had partners, job that big. Well, well — not another word."

Fifty thousand dollars was more than a man needed to live on his entire life. But how many fortunes that size would fit into *mine,* if Uncle Jim didn't mess it up? Because I still believed the Slicks — too much money was involved *not* to. Anyway, figuring my share at $50 million? I was a *thousand times* richer than the yeggman!

As I tried to suppress a smirk, Frank Holloway looked at me sweetly.

"Want to rob banks when you grow up, son?"

"*No.* Why would I?"

"Oh, it's fun. Keeps your mind tuned, and gives good men

like your uncle work. Pay's not bad, neither."

The waitress brought us our meal—no need to take our order, we always had the Blue Plate special. Tonight it was chicken-fried pork, okra, mashed potatoes with gravy. Frank Holloway looked pityingly at our plates and said to her, "On my tab, honey."

"*Not* on your tab," said Uncle Jim. "Got that, Wilma?"

"Yes, Sheriff."

"Sorry," Frank Holloway said humbly, eyes glittering. He enjoyed baiting my uncle, I realized.

Now he nodded at the Slicks, who were just getting to their feet.

"Say, Sheriff, congratulations on your New York fortune. Millions for nothing! Should have chosen *my* parents more carefully. And here I thought your people were just dirt farmers!

"Oh, he's not talking to me," he continued, addressing me while Uncle Jim did his best Comanche. "Bear no ill will, won't you tell him? Fact, on his advice, looking for honest work myself: Headed to Hollywood. Tom Mix a movie star? Move over, the Oklahoma Yeggman's coming to town!"

"Ask him," Uncle Jim said—to *me!*—"why they picked him up a common pickpocket?"

"Tell him it concerned an affair of the heart I can't go into. Wouldn't care to besmirch a lady's name." Frank Holloway glared at the woman sitting beside him.

"Wondered about that," Uncle Jim remarked. "Tell him, I wondered about that."

8.

NEXT DAY AT SCHOOL, after another night spending my millions — despite Uncle Jim's cold water — I could hardly keep my eyes open as the teacher droned on about how they make visitors to the Alamo speak in whispers, when I saw the Sheriff's Model T speed past the school and turn in at the train platform. Rube leapt out and ran into the stationmaster's shack.

Without thinking, I stood up and rushed out of the classroom and out of school towards it, ignoring shouts behind me. When Rube ran out again and sped past me back towards the jailhouse, I changed direction and ran the whole way after him. When I got there, the Model T was angled in the street, chugging away, and Rube and Uncle Jim just hustling out carrying Winchester rifles.

I climbed in back, and no one shooed me off. Rube gunned it.

"Uncle Jim, *what's happening?*"

"Bank's been robbed," he said over his shoulder. "Down in Harrold."

"*Robbed?* Who did it?"

"Who you think?"

Thrilling! Heading for the scene of the crime with my uncles, out of school *again!* Rough ride over a rutted road, but I was happy as a hound dog with tongue and ears flapping in the cool breeze.

"Left word," Rube said. "Tries boarding a train, won't hinder him, but they'll let Willie know."

"Good," said Uncle Jim.

Snuggling down, I watched the countryside stream past in dun shades beneath the coconut-macaroon sky. At one well-watered stretch, barbed wire protected what looked like snowfields.

Uncle Jim pointed at them.

"Cotton, Bing. Harvest next month. New these past few years, but there's money in it.

"When I was a boy and barbed wire first came in? Any farmer try to fence in rangeland, make fields out of it, we'd go out at night, snip it between the posts. Groveses were *cattlemen*."

A column of dust arose ahead of us, a brown plume with edges feathering southeast. That meant it was coming towards us.

"Someone," said Rube.

Two minutes later Uncle Jim yelled, "Holy *Hell!* Stop the car, Rube! Block the road!"

He did it, but the oncoming car merely circled around us. It was a yellow Pierce-Arrow, grille aglitter with slantwise chrome lettering, going Hell for leather. Beautiful machine! In the excitement none of us could make out who was driving, except that he wore a leather helmet and isinglass goggles.

"*Shit!*" yelled Uncle Jim, and to me: "Sorry, son."

"Chase it?" Rube asked.

"No, on to Harrold. There's no catching a Pierce-Arrow."

Harrold turned out to be a crossroads of low wooden buildings, except for the bank on one corner, a columned limestone temple that seemed a remnant of Imperial Rome, only by grievous happenstance being attached not to arcaded palaces but to a feed store on one side, on the other a stable. Its high, barred windows bore gold lettering. On the slate sidewalk stood a man in a three-piece suit, hands on hips.

Rube stopped the car, Uncle Jim jumped out and brushed past the man into the bank, and by the time I caught up with him was on the telephone telling the Vernon city marshals Frank Holloway was on his way in a yellow Pierce-Arrow, watch the streets, hotel, train platform, stop any vehicle going faster than the "slow lope" that was the official speed limit.

Then he returned outdoors.

"Well, sir?" he asked the man in the suit, who was the bank manager.

"Should have kept him locked up, Sheriff!"

"Frank Holloway?"

"Waltzes in *by* his lonesome, Colt in each fist, says hand it over. Just like last year!"

"How much he get?"

"Near $14,000!"

"How'd he get away?"

"Same way he got here, by Pierce-Arrow automobile!"

"Which direction?"

"Lit out for Vernon!"

Sighing, Uncle Jim stepped indoors again. It was a handsome room, with polished floor, marble counter and a brass grille behind which a tall safe stood open and empty. A lady cashier was sobbing on her stool. Confirming that the bank was as empty of clues as of money, he didn't need to see more.

"Won't get away this time," he told the manager. Then we piled back into the Model T and Uncle Jim told Rube to take us to Niggertown.

"Don't imagine even Frank Holloway would parade through Vernon in a yellow car," he said.

Every town in Texas has its Niggertown near by. Don't like the word—Ma banned it in our house, where Brazil nuts were Brazil nuts—but that's what it's always called. Vernon's was a mile this side, where the ground broke up into shelves and draws, not much good for anything, just one unpaved block with houses built by freed slaves and occupied by them and their families. When the Sheriff's T turned into it, several residents vanished from the street, while others appeared at their doors.

"Try Jumbles' Garage," said Uncle Jim, and Rube nosed in at the end of the block, in front of closed barn doors. Later they told me Jumbles Slaughter was known to dabble in shady stuff from time to time. Mr. Slaughter stepped out with impassive dignity as Uncle Jim dashed up.

Asking, "Mind?" my uncle swung one door open, revealing a yellow Pierce-Arrow parked inside. Even from the T we could hear the engine still ticking.

"Where is he, uncle?" he asked.

"No idea," said Mr. Slaughter. "Paid to park this. Borrowed my T. Paid for that, too."

"Which way'd he go?"

Mr. Slaughter indicated Vernon.

Uncle Jim gave the street a look — went over it, stooping.

"Your T open or closed?" he called as he got back in ours. We knew the color — Model Ts were black.

"Closed."

Rube pulled out in a rush, saying, "Jim, he'll be going *north*: Vernon to *Elmer* to *Altus*, then maybe Caney, *Kansas*."

Even I had heard of Caney, Kansas, a border town notorious for wanted men evading their pursuers.

"Maybe," said Uncle Jim.

"Or *south*, Jim!" said Rube. "That's where *I'd* go — San Antone, even the border. That's it, Jim, the *border!*"

"Turn in at Wedgie Taylor's, Rube," said Uncle Jim. To me he said, "Bing, favor to ask. Want you to go up and look for a closed Model T with Frank Holloway driving it."

"*Up?*" I asked in confusion, just as we came off the road alongside a square barn with an aeroplane standing in front of it — a two-seat Curtiss Jenny. At the far end of a meadow a windsock hung sideways, pretty well filled.

By great good luck, Mr. Taylor himself was carrying a jerry can away from the plane. I'm talking about a wood-and-fabric biplane of the sort my parents wouldn't in a million years have let me board! Uncle Jim was out of the car before it stopped, yelling at me to follow, and when I reached him was telling Mr. Taylor, "—not half an hour ago, so not far whatever direction, just waggle your wings and we'll follow."

Looking at me, Mr. Taylor drawled, "Yeah, I'll find him a helmet," and with exasperating slowness carried the can into the barn.

"Been up myself," Uncle Jim told me. "Perfectly safe in Wedgie's hands."

Mr. Taylor came out and pulled goggles and helmet over my head. Boosting me over a strut and into the front seat, he fastened canvas belts across my chest and clambered into the seat behind. I was startled to find controls in front of me, but fortunately there was a second set in front of him.

"All right, Jim, prop 'er!" he yelled. *"Contact!"*

Putting his back into it, Uncle Jim pushed at the propeller.

Didn't catch, though.

I heard Mr. Taylor toggle a switch and again yell, *"Contact!"* and Uncle Jim pushed. This time the engine sputtered, caught and roared.

My uncles ducked to remove chocks from the wheels. Rube being quicker at it, the plane instantly wheeled round, Mr. Taylor corrected, aimed us at the windsock, and as we passed it we were sailing tentatively up into the air and gently coming to earth again. Up; down; up, up, *up*. Best sensation of my whole life! Kite-like, we bounded into the air, negotiating with wind and gravity for every foot of altitude, engine working hard and beginning to win.

Bounding higher, tantalizingly close to the puffball clouds, we commenced circling. Vernon was a gray-and-brown tablecloth laid on the countryside's checkerboard; people were *ants*. Feeling no fear — though I can't explain why — I went to work scouring the roads around it. Straight, mostly following section lines, they weren't exactly teeming with traffic, but I could see a number of horse-drawn wagons, buggies and automobiles, including some open Model Ts; but no closed ones.

Could also see the ford at Doan's Crossing, where, the banks falling away, the Red River widens and slows. Ma's first job teaching was in its two-room schoolhouse, from which she saw the last great herds of 25,000 or even 50,000 cattle crossing in a day, wading and swimming in hump-backed fields of brown.

Cattlemen would pool their herds and drive them past Vernon up the Western Trail — the Chisholm's local branch — to sell in Dodge City or Kansas City. Cowboys would pack the saloons that lined the courthouse square, spoiling both for women — especially the fancy ones in houses tucked near the railroad tracks — and fights, doing their best to raise Hell from down below to Vernon's streets! Most carried six-shooters, some without triggers — guns that fired with just a lift of thumb on hammer. Ma said Gram, tiny as she was, used to sally outdoors with her broom and break up cowboy fights in the street.

Mr. Taylor plucking my shoulder, I went back to work, scanning the ground as we made a higher, wider circle. Briefly we found a world of brilliant silver pastures, before dropping beneath the clouds again and going northwest over a dirt track that paralleled the railway.

Plucking at me again, Mr. Taylor pointed north. At the horizon was a band of darkness that looked out of place.

"Tell your uncles," he shouted. "Blue norther's coming. Let's try south."

But I chopped my hand northwest and he complied, however

skeptically, and a minute later we overtook a closed Model T, our speed so much greater that it seemed a doodlebug squashed into the terrain. But it was the one: I was sure of it when, as we buzzed him, the mustachioed driver shook his fist at us: It was the yeggman.

In fact the car was moving smartly along, wheels blurred within clouds of dust.

"There he is!" I yelled. *"Higher,* Mr. Taylor! Waggle your wings!" And higher we went, madly waggling our wings. Holding on tight, I twisted around to look for my uncles' car, found it and saw it turn. Mr. Taylor was banking to go home when I shouted, "Put me on the road, Mr. Taylor."

"But—"

"Please put me down to wait for my uncles. *Please!"*

And in we went for the landing a few hundred yards ahead of the T. No sooner had I scrambled out than, engine roaring, the Jenny took off again and Frank Holloway came tearing past as if I weren't there. Had to jump in the ditch.

Regaining the road, I stood there watching that weather come my way and taking in its wonderful topsoil smell. Why does dirt smell so good, anyhow? It was getting cold. By the time the Sheriff's T came speeding up, I was jumping up and down for warmth. It stopped, and I got in.

"Got him, Uncle Jim! He's just ahead!"

"Good work, Bing!"

"Mr. Taylor says a blue norther's coming."

They glanced north. What from the air had been a distant band of steel-blue was already forebodingly close.

"Oh, Hell. All we need."

"What's a blue norther?"

"You'll see," said Uncle Jim. "Bad news for us."

Perched on the backseat, I was still swooping through the sky—most fun *ever!*—while my uncles conferred. When we reached a crossroads a sign identified as Chillicothe, Pop. 268, Uncle Jim said, "This'll do, Rube."

Rube stopped the car and Uncle Jim clambered out. "Come on, Bing. Rube, catch you up soon as we can. Catch *him,* all the better."

"Do my best," said Rube, and drove on down the road.

"Bing, you and I are going back to Vernon to raise a posse."

"*Posse?*" I asked.

"*Posse comitatus,*" Uncle Jim answered. "First in years. But Frank Holloway has a start and a car, so we need all the help we can get. Should have done it after he robbed that damn bank the first time."

9.

UNCLE JIM FOUND a telephone at a blacksmith's and started Aunt Willie spreading the word about needing men and cars. Told her we'd flag down the next train — a freight, but Uncle Jim said the engineer would give us a lift — and be there soon as we could.

But the smithy insisted on driving us back.

As we got there we saw men flocking towards the jail, where others already milled. The storm hadn't hit town yet, but the temperature was dropping dramatically.

"OK, people," Uncle Jim bellowed from the steps. "Our yeggman's gone and robbed that same damn bank again. He's fleeing into the Panhandle, and Rube's on his tail, already past Chillicothe. Looking for a dozen volunteers and four fast cars to go bring him back!"

Men clamored to be chosen. The most excitement anybody had seen in years!

"All right, good, Fred, thanks," said Uncle Jim, pointing. "Clete, got your Maxwell? Fine! Ten minutes, right here."

His dozen chosen, he went indoors, found Aunt Willie's Bible and grabbed a handful of flimsy six-pointed tin stars with pins on the back (I still have mine). Also he took cash from his office safe, opened the gun case and reverently lifted out the half dozen Winchester rifles in it and filled my arms with ammunition. We used the john, took Aunt Willie's sacks of bread-and-jelly sandwiches, and were set.

Until Uncle Eustace barged in.

"Jim, got four new Willys-Knight touring cars for you," he said. "Extra gas, extra tires. Be here straightaway."

"No time to wait, Eustace."

"Insist, Jim, I *insist*. Trove of publicity, and you can't trust a Maxwell — *you* know that."

They bickered and dickered in the way of brothers, and Uncle Jim had to give in. While waiting he handed out his stars and swore us on the Bible; suspect he made up the oath in his own head. Also he handed out Winchesters. There were only enough rifles for half the men, but the others, lifting their coattails or patting their pockets, made clear we had firepower enough regardless. Uncle Jim's own rifle sported something I never saw before, a gunsight carved from bone.

"No glare in the sun," he explained when I asked why.

But then, maddeningly, once the Willys-Knights drove up nose to tail — Uncle Clois driving one — and we'd stowed our weapons and supplies and were taking our seats, Uncle Eustace made us get out again so Vernon's veteran photographer could take a picture.

"Need that photograph," he said tersely. "Not charging for the vehicles, am I?"

The photographer's boy ran up carrying an old-fashioned bellows camera with cape and tripod, his self-important boss striding behind him. Assessing the light — the front pushing through made it dark — the old man directed the camera's placement, posing everybody against the cars while he stooped under the cape and took the photograph that hangs in the Sheriff's Department to this day. (The open-mouthed blur dancing from foot to foot like he needs the bathroom, though really it's to urge, *"Get a move on!"*? That's me.)

With that, we were off. Uncle Jim hulked in the passenger seat of the lead Willys-Knight, his brother Eustace driving. I sat between two big men in the backseat, where there wasn't much room amongst gas cans and extra tires.

By now it was miserably cold, and as we headed out of town the skies opened up and began peppering us — *salting* us — with hailstones the size of golf balls that puckered our canvas roofs. Above us it had gone blue — dark blue, not sky-blue. The hailstorm finally relented, changing to snow as we paralleled the train tracks, passing cotton fields already crystalline. Its dirt and gravel catching the hailstones, the road was slick with ice and, our tires slipping, we yawed back and forth about as far as we went forward. But Frank Holloway would find the going just as tough.

As we passed Chillicothe it was darker behind us than in front, though snow continued.

Half an hour onwards, we came upon a sad sight. My uncle Rube — shivering, desolated, refusing to look at us — stood leaning against Frank Holloway's Model T, which, one wheel off, nuzzled the ground as though asleep. His own car — the Sheriff's official vehicle — was nowhere to be seen, nor was the yeggman. The road unspooled empty to the horizon.

"All right, Rube," Uncle Jim said gently, laying a hand on his shoulder.

"Had him, Jim. Had him right here. Broke down — bump took his wheel clear off. Said a wheel went spinning past and he just had time to wonder whose in Hell it could be when down goes his car. I come along, he's siphoning gasoline into cans. Put my Colt on him, told him to stop right there."

"I know, Rube, I know."

"Dammit, Jim, *had* him. Tells me what happened while he stows his cans in your T, then gets in and drives off like he knows I'll never shoot."

"All right, Rube, all right."

"*Dammit,* Jim."

It was embarrassing, Rube catching up to Frank Holloway but letting him take his car off him and get away. There was muttering about it, too, but even I knew you had to forgive him.

I knew because the day I arrived in Vernon the first thing I asked my Uncle Jim was, "Uncle Jim, did you ever shoot anybody?"

"*Wa-al,* no, never needed to," came his disappointing answer. "Thank God."

"*Ohh!*" I said, cast down.

But I perked up at his next words: "Now, don't you go asking your uncle Reuben that question."

"Why not?"

And of course he had to tell me why not. Uncle Jim never treated me like a kid, and rightly figured that if he didn't tell me, I (being a kid) would go ask Rube and make him feel worse about what made him feel bad every day of his life.

Because he had. Shot someone, I mean, and killed him, too. It was a boy and accidental.

This was ten years earlier, when Rube was deputy city marshal in Altus, Oklahoma, the next sizable town to the north.

New Year's Eve, he was patrolling the square, its saloons raucous with life, from all sides shots going into the air, when a minute after midnight bullets whizzed past his head. By reflex he turned and fired into the darkness, drilling the mayor's son through the heart.

Striking a match, Rube saw him take his last breaths, panic in the eyes until their lights went out. The boy, just 17 years old, was still holding the gun he'd fired blindly into the darkness to celebrate the New Year. Rube was devastated. He knew him, a lanky, good-looking kid who liked to laugh.

They buried him in the town cemetery.

Mayor's son? The grand jury indicted Rube for murder.

While awaiting trial he was reassigned to Elmer, a hamlet south of town with a second-story marshal's station, and there had another adventure: One day he arrested a black resident on the charge of rape, and that evening a torch-waving mob came up to demand the prisoner be turned over to it. Rube sent the slow-talking jailer out front to stall them, while he snuck the prisoner down the back stairs and onto a horse that carried them to Altus.

The jury found Rube not guilty—Ma said it didn't hurt having his brothers sit in the front row, arms crossed, glaring at the jurymen—but he resigned and came home to Vernon, where Jim insisted he become his deputy. They both knew his shooting days were over, but Uncle Jim, never having needed to shoot anyone himself, didn't see it as disqualifying.

"Sorry, Jim. Should have plugged him when I had him."

"You hush. We'll get him."

Rube taking the wheel of our car, Uncle Eustace commandeered the next one behind.

10.

THE SNOW STOPPED, the temperature started to rise and everything melted into mud.

Crossing the Texas Panhandle by train, I'd marveled at its endlessness. Now it seemed bigger still. The colors poking out of the snow varied from a kind of remembrance of green to golds with all brightness leached away. Terns, tanagers and blackbirds leapt from stalk to stalk or gyred in masses overhead before dissolving back to earth, and flights of geese honked their way south. While the snow still blew, cattle huddled in the lee of insignificant rises or minute rills. After it stopped, they grazed at whatever poked through the white as though nothing had happened.

And never a fence; Uncle Jim said it was the last open range he knew. Horizon to horizon made an enormous platter you could see everything in.

You hear "posse," you think men on horseback searching out subtle clues to the trail, broken twigs or stirred-up dirt. Wasn't like that for us, not at that point. There was a road, however rough, our prey's tire tracks plain enough. Though we had to stop occasionally to change tires or gas up from our cans, we made good progress.

Rube asked Uncle Jim where he thought the yeggman was headed, and Uncle Jim said, "For tonight, the Duke's."

"The Duke's!"

"Knows he'll be safe there."

I knew about dukes. I'd read *Ivanhoe* over the summer, and *The Three Musketeers*.

Rube ventured, "Get a good meal."

The others grinned in agreement. Uncle Jim just sighed, but finally said, "And warm."

No one explained anything, leaving me perplexed as we persevered. The sky was a uniform gray, except where the descending sun bashed it silver as briefly it emerged, to be dunked out of sight at the horizon.

Meanwhile, a speck appeared off to the left. It got bigger, began to look interesting, and in the middle of nowhere our procession—along with the telephone poles—turned towards it, the yeggman's tracks still leading the way. Soon we passed between gateposts supporting an arch that spelled out *Castle Fairplay* in wrought-iron curlicues.

As we got closer, the speck revealed itself to be a log house built on a grand scale. Smoke wreathed upwards from numerous chimneys, light against the dark sky. Windows glittered with lamplight and, behind a stone tower, slate roofs rose over high log walls.

"It's a *castle!*" I said in wonder.

"Sure enough," Uncle Jim said. "Duke's an old friend, he'll put us up for the night. Only thing," he added, craning round to look at me, "he calls it his duchy—Duchy of Fairplay—and his rules apply. So if you see Frank Holloway, just be polite."

Confounding though this was, when we pulled up in the forecourt there was the yeggman's car—rather, the stolen Sheriff's Department Model T—parked out front, poised for escape. Up a flight of stairs at the base of the tower, double doors opened and two men marched out. Astoundingly, they wore *skirts* and carried bags bristling with udders. Blowing and pulling on these produced a caterwauling that carried across the plain.

Oh, I got it: kilts and bagpipes.

A smiling, compact man in a tartan jacket with silken lapels came through the door and shambled halfway down the steps.

"That you, Jim? Rube? Eustace and Clois, too! Glad you made it. Expecting you, you know. Welcome to Castle Fairplay, everybody," he said in a funny voice. It was the first English accent I ever heard.

"Thank you, m'lud," Uncle Jim called. "This is Bing, our sister's boy."

"Bing, welcome," mine host said kindly.

"Thank you."

"Thank you, *m'lud*," Uncle Jim prompted.

"Thank you, your *grace*," I said, knowing the entitlement of dukes.

But this one laughed and said, "No, no, that's my brother, I'm merely Lord Aloysius, *m'lud* will do." He winked at me. "This might be the prettiest lad I ever saw!"

Standing before us was one of the Texas Panhandle's authentic historical treasures. The second son of the next-to-premier duke of England retired from Her Majesty's army in 1887 satiated with the blood of Africans and African game, lived it up in London for a few years, friends with Oscar Wilde and his circle, then thought it best to buy some 190,000 acres in Texas, and settled there, never to leave. Built his castle and raised his cattle. At first he hunted, but soon found he'd had enough even of shooting pheasant. He had cropped white hair, long auburn mustaches and big, unhappy eyes.

"Come in, come in, always glad of the company," he was saying as the posse trooped past. "We've another guest, as I'm sure you suspect, and I'll remind you of the rules of hospitality here at Castle Fairplay."

"Of course, m'lud," Uncle Jim murmured.

"Ruler of his own domain," our host said as if to himself. Then: "Know Frank Holloway, I believe?"

And standing inside the door, smiling and dapper, was the Oklahoma Yeggman.

"Jim. Rube. *Bing.*"

"Frank."

Wondrous though this was, I was even more taken with the hall we stepped into. It stretched into the distance, rafters and wagon-wheel electroliers high overhead, lacquered log walls, mounted buffalo, lion and elephant trophies, enormous fireplaces snapping at logs of pinyon pine. Everything smelled invitingly of wood, beeswax, leather, brass polish. At either end broad staircases rose to a balcony that overlooked the whole.

"*Wow!*" I exclaimed. "Love your castle, m'lud!"

"Oh course he loves it. And I love *him*. Love to spoil him. Wonder if he'd let me spoil him? Earl, will you show everybody to their rooms? And then we dine."

We followed his man upstairs and along the balcony as he assigned the rooms opening off it two by two, then led Uncle Jim and me into a marvelous chamber with two beds whose silk hangings reflected the jollity of the fire.

"Thanks, Earl," Uncle Jim said.

Saying, "Drinks before dinner," the cowboy left.

"He's an *earl?*" I asked, ready to believe anything.

"Naw, that's his name: Earl Johnson."

After washing up in a bathroom of oversized porcelain fixtures, Uncle Jim opened a closet and, pursing his lips, chose our dinner suits: for himself a dark-green jacket, for me blue velvet with white flounces. Made me feel like Little Lord Fauntleroy, but I loved it: A foretaste of my life after the Claim went through and I built myself a castle bigger than the Duke's!

We met Rube and the others on the balcony and marched

downstairs.

"Yes, yes, quite right—no ceremony at Castle Fairplay," the Duke called as we came up. Now in black tie, glass in hand, he was warming his backside at the center mantel. He focused on me. "My, *my!* Prettier at every glance. How lips—so ruby red!—impress one as wishing to be pressed with one's own."

My uncles and their friends poured Tennessee whiskey at a sideboard, but the Duke handed me a glass of ginger beer. My first; I liked the way bubbles came out my nose.

Splendid in black and silver, Frank Holloway got himself some whiskey, too.

"Nice chase you led us," Uncle Jim remarked.

Before the yeggman could respond, our host closed his eyes in pain and raised a palm.

"No shop talk, *please.*"

"Sorry, m'lud," said Uncle Jim.

It was pleasant, and certainly novel, to cap off an exhausting day with such an evening. At the Duke's invitation, I crept onto his red-leather Chesterfield couch beside the fire, and was surprised when he woke me up from a dream of the Cheshire Cat to find Frank Holloway's eyes burning into me.

We went into dinner. The dining room—banqueting hall—was straight out of Sir Walter Scott: long, polished table and, hanging on high, regimental banners and six Texas flags.

"Anywhere they like," our host said, taking his place at the head. "No ceremony at Castle Fairplay."

My uncles and our dozen and myself took seats near his end, as Frank Holloway, Earl, the bagpipers and other Duke's men joined us. Quite a crowd, all told. Two cowboys brought out platters piled with steaks and potatoes, and handed them round before sitting down themselves.

The meat was succulent and delicious.

"Does the boy like his buffalo steak?" m'lud wondered. "Oh

yes, keep a herd, little herd, thousand head or so. Buffalo's good for you. Show 'em to you, if you can stay. Usually over on the creek this time of year. Can he stay, Jim, be my page? Had a page in Ethiopia black as ebony. *Beautiful.*"

"No, m'lud," said Uncle Jim.

Nodding, the Duke addressed the length of the table.

"I think Lord Carnarvon's discovery of King Tutankhamen's tomb a suitable topic for dinner conversation. Yes, a *very* good topic."

This spectacular event had just taken place, Howard Carter chiseling a peephole through the tomb's door and answering Carnarvon's query, "Can you see anything?" with, "Yes, *wonderful* things."

"Lucky Carnarvon," m'lud said (of course this was before King Tut's curse killed him), and went on to speak learnedly of scarabs, sarcophagi and mummification, dwelling as we ate on how they sucked the brains out through the nostrils, and how really he should get some mummies of his own, stand them in the hall in their cases of enamel and gold.

"Don't see the point myself," remarked Uncle Jim. "Give me a grave dug in good honest dirt any day."

Our host looked at him speculatively.

"Wouldn't care for my family mausoleum, Jim. Built into a hillside — marble façade, bronze doors, shelves for fifty coffins."

"No, thanks," agreed my uncle.

"Well, may be right. Food for worms, after all — that's our lot, isn't it?"

"I'm going to build a mausoleum like yours, m'lud," I announced. "I am, too, Uncle Jim, for your father and your sister Nelly and everyone."

Didn't volunteer how I was going to pay for it, though. Everyone laughed, but uneasily.

The Duke addressed me.

"Your grandparents and I had a mutual friend, did you know? Quanah, Chief of the Comanche?"

Ma had told me about him. Quanah Parker, son of a Comanche warrior and the white woman he kidnapped, grew up to be their chief and helped them tail off their war on the whites (though the whites' war on them continued). A landowner and rancher, he used to visit my grandparents on Beaver Creek, dying about the time I was born.

"Great man, Quanah," Uncle Jim remarked. "Know the story of President Roosevelt's coming through Vernon to go hunting on his ranch, m'lud? They're up there at Star House one night, and T.R. mentions the one thing white people hold against Quanah: That he has so many wives. Four at the time, down from seven or eight. T.R. tells him whites'd like him better if he cast off all but one."

"*And?*" asked the Duke, smiling.

"Oh, Quanah agreed right off. Said, 'I'll *do* it, Mr. President, keep just one wife — if *you* tell the other three.'"

They guffawed and, taking my hand, the Duke led me back to the couch beside the fire.

Now, with his tacit approval, the talk turned shop.

Uncle Jim asked, "So you had to go down to Harrold and do it again, Frank?"

"After that outrageous bond Judge Ohlmacher set?"

"You'll get five years, easy."

Frank Holloway smiled a smile full of hate. "*If* you catch me."

"Oh, we'll do that, don't you doubt it. By the way, can't let you take my car in the morning."

"Not taking any car," said Frank Holloway with great good humor. "Our host has horses for us all."

"My idea," the Duke said. "Want to see one last old-time posse. And Frank deserves a sportin' chance, Jim — hour's head start."

"Yes, m'lud."

"Welcome to any mounts you like, pick of my stables."

"Thank you, m'lud."

Yawning at the fire, I heard no more.

11.

WOKE UP IN SHEETS smelling of sunshine, slices of sun gilding the floor. Uncle Jim's bed was empty.

He opened the door and peremptorily called, "Five minutes, Bing, breakfast in the car. *Move* it."

Car? Yawning, I tumbled into that wonderful bathroom, tumbled out and looked over the railing while buttoning my shirt. The Duke, Uncle Jim, Rube, Eustace, Clois and the rest of the posse were just going out the door. My uncles looked grim and upset.

I walked downstairs and out between the bagpipers. Saw fine horses being led up on one side, to the other the freshly-washed Sheriff's Model T, the Duke himself stowing gas cans as Uncle Jim got behind the wheel and motioned to me.

Clois and Eustace crowding him, Rube started to say, "Tell us –" His voice cracked.

As he stepped on the starter, Uncle Jim said softly, "I'll take care of him. Find him and bring him home, you can be sure of that. Good luck, everybody! Thanks, m'lud."

Turning out of the forecourt and lunging down the muddy road, we left the way we'd come. After passing under the iron archway and turning towards Vernon, Uncle Jim gave me a look of woe.

"Sorry about breakfast." Between us was a paper sack, which he shoved closer to me.

"Uncle Jim, what's *happened?*"

"Biscuits. Eat. Earl gave 'em to us. We'll join 'em soon as we can, Bing, be in at the kill, most likely — I mean when they take Frank Holloway — but something we have to do first."

"*What?*"

"Telephone call this morning."

He didn't say anything else, but his face was working. Alarmed at seeing tears gather, I shut up, afraid to hear whatever might come next.

It didn't come for a long time. I'd eaten some biscuits, and we were jouncing along the track alongside the FW&DC and telephone poles, when Uncle Jim spoke in a thick voice.

"You know I was a little boy — younger'n you — when your grandfather died," he stated, and cleared his throat.

"Yes, two weeks before Ma was born," I said. "She never knew him."

"That's right. Fever took his 2-year-old, Nelly, out on Beaver Creek, and then him. Well, we buried them next to each other in the cemetery there. Ansley Cemetery they used to call it. Now they call it Four Corners, I don't know why."

"Why'd they call it Ansley Cemetery?"

He flashed a smile. "Don't know that, either."

"I've seen it, Uncle Jim. You took me out there. It's pretty. Those cottonwoods, and he has a nice stone — that marble carved with the compass and dove. It's a pretty place." I was speaking as persuasively as I could, and it seemed to calm him.

He sighed and said, "Never heard the like, Bing. They telephoned this morning to say his grave's been opened."

"*Opened?*"

He turned hollow eyes on me. "And it's empty. Someone's taken your grandfather's body."

I had the feeling Ma called someone walking on your grave. *Literally!* I was shocked — felt malevolence reach into my chest and eviscerate me. *Why?* Why my grandfather? Why *him?*

Why *us?*

"Who did it?" I asked.

"No idea, none a-tall. Who'd snatch a *body?*"

That's when Uncle Jim explained: Grave robbery's taking *things* out of a grave, but when the *body's* taken, it's body snatching.

He'd heard of it only one time before.

"Geronimo. Buried up at Fort Sill, where he died?" Fort Sill's in Oklahoma, near Altus. "Few years ago some soldiers outraged the tomb – stole Geronimo's skull and jewelry. Imagine how low down you'd have to be to do a thing like *that?* Rich grave, probably – something like King Tut's, I imagine. Easterner did it. Eastern scum named Prescott Bush."

It was near noon by the time we passed my grandfather's old place, planks and posts silver with age. The cemetery wasn't much further. We pulled up beneath its trees. A few wagons and cars were out front, people standing beside them, eyes lighted up with excitement. A nervous city marshal kept them outside the gate.

We walked through, Uncle Jim scanning faces and the ground.

"Hey, Brady," he called to the marshal.

"Sheriff," said Brady. "Well, the good thing is two Waggoner hands happened to ride past at sunup, noticed this mess. Could have been days, otherwise."

Uncle Jim nodded grimly. Following, I sucked in my breath. My grandfather's tombstone lay broken into three pieces, and mounds of dirt rose beside a gaping chasm in the ground. Teetering on the edge, I looked into a deep, dark hole.

"Careful, Bing," Uncle Jim said. "Not last night, anyway: No prints in the mud. But recent. Night before last, maybe." He called, "My ma know about this?"

"Fetching her now."

Sighing, steadying himself with both arms, my uncle jumped

into the grave. It was full six-feet deep and black as night. Only part of his head emerged.

"Deep, boy oh boy, it's *deep*." Stooping, he felt around and, coming to his feet, held a handful of mud up to the light. From it he plucked a coffin handle half rusted away and, holding it out to me, murmured, "Daddy might have made this himself."

Every time he bent down he took a deep breath as if plunging into water, and looked dizzy and nauseous when he came up for air. Apparently not a comfortable thing to do, rooting around in your father's grave.

Standing up again, he spat in his hand and rubbed something into Masonic colors.

"Remember Ma pinning this to his breast," he said of the enamel emblem.

He turned to the grave's other end and, bobbing out of sight, with an exclamation picked something up out of the dirt and lofted it: a bone, brown and dirty.

"Tibia," he said, tenderly laying it down. "Left? *Left* shinbone, do believe."

Lifting another handful, he poked at it and I glimpsed white: toe bones or foot bones. But aside from more coffin-handle fragments, nails and celluloid buttons — and a hank of hair that he picked up and put down again without saying anything — that was it. No wood, no fabric, no more bones. Everything else was gone or turned to dust. I'd never felt so empty.

Another city marshal drove a Model T up to the gate. Gram sat up front. After being helped down, she came through in her long dress with lace-trimmed apron and bonnet and went over to her husband's open grave.

Uncle Jim climbed out of it and made to embrace her, but she spied that shinbone and leaned down to pick it up. Clutching it like a scepter, she kissed it.

"This all of him, Jim?"

"'Fraid so, Ma. Careful, don't get too close. And this." He handed her the Masonic pin, which she scrutinized while we braced ourselves for a flood of tears. But no tears came. Her eyes stayed as dry as her parchment skin. So did mine, whereas Uncle Jim kept bringing his arm up to clear his.

"Jim, who did this?"

"I'll get 'em, Ma—promise."

"*Who?*"

"I'll find out, Ma," he said, "and make 'em sorry they were ever born."

Gram looked at the mounds and said, "You'll sift the dirt?"

"Every grain."

"This time we'll bury him in East View, pour cement over him."

Gram returned to the car holding that bone to her bosom.

"Cement," Uncle Jim said to me. "Like Billy the Kid. Well, guess we have to." He asked Brady, "Anything we can sift this dirt with?"

Brady eagerly asked around, and someone hastened to a Model T truck and, improbably pulling out a framed piece of screening, brought it over with a shovel. Uncle Jim said thanks.

Lowering himself into the grave, he painstakingly lifted dirt shovelful by shovelful from the bottom and dropped it over the screen. Found a few more buttons and nails that way. Wouldn't let me help.

"Right and proper for a son to do this for his father," he remarked.

"Ma says in India when they burn the body, the son has to bash in his father's skull to let the soul escape."

Uncle Jim looked startled. "*Well,*" he said.

Climbing out of the hole, he began sifting the dirt from the mounds back into it. That laborious process—he did let me relieve him a few times—yielded nothing. When we were done, I stamped down the grave while he went to look for footprints and other traces outside the gates. Not finding any, we loaded up, said goodbye to Marshal Brady and Jim aimed the car for Vernon.

"Who do you think did it, Uncle Jim?"

"Who *would* do such a thing, Bing? Who hates us so much? Feels personal—*very* personal—and I really had no idea anyone despised me—*us*—quite that bad."

"Maybe it's money?" I ventured.

He laughed. "Always a guess, but where's the money here?"

"Was it the yeggman?"

"Don't think so. Not his style."

It was a handsome November afternoon, completely unlike the day before, the blue norther's ice and snow forgotten as if they never were. Barreling past cotton fields where farmers with long faces were assessing the damage, Uncle Jim exclaimed, "Oh, *Hell!*"

A minute later: *"Shit!* Like a goddam story you'd tell to *children!*"

"What, Uncle Jim?"

"Oh, just doing a bit of first-rate detective work over here, Bing. Some real Sherlock Holmes stuff. Which a Texas sheriff doesn't get to do every day of the week, believe me. You put me on to it with your 'money.' Makes me ashamed.

"Lay it out for you: Someone's taken Nathan Micajah Groves's bones, all but a shinbone." A gasp or sob momentarily took him, but he let it settle down. "Now, who was just telling us about a one-legged pirate named Nathan Micajah Groves?"

I corrected him: *"Privateer."*

"Which leg did they say got shot off?"

Left leg. "I forget," I said.

Could it be? The legal papers would prove the Claim. What could *bones* add?

"I think the Slicks—" Uncle Jim began. "Mind you, don't think they dug up that grave themselves. Had someone do the dirty work for them. Think that was my idiot nephews — that damn Harry and Ginger. Where'd we find 'em, this time of day?"

"Harry'll be at the dealership," I said. "Ginger's probably out digging some cellar or other."

"How that boy loves to dig," Jim muttered.

"But Uncle Jim, the Groves Claim —"

"*Hush!*" he said fiercely. "Bing, what's so offensive is that those men are *crooks*. Con men. Made up that Claim business out of whole cloth, or the next thing to it, to try and get some easy money. That's all they care about. Looked for greedy folk, and when they met your cousins knew they had themselves some live ones. Hit pay dirt with Harry and Ginger!"

Well, the scales fell from my eyes. Uncle Jim was right, and I saw it. Painful to have my dreams evaporate, disintegrate, dissolve, to grieve for my lost fortune, my charities, too, to mourn the mansion with columns and solarium I now couldn't buy Ma. And felt sick that her father was *gone*.

SOON, COMING INTO the outskirts of town, houses were crowding up against commercial buildings. Public square to the left, the dealership was straight ahead. Uncle Jim parked askew in front of it. Law enforcement likes to do that, stress the hurry they're in, how important their business is (won't let you do it, though).

He strode indoors, boots heavy on the tile, and startled Harry and Ginger sitting at Harry's desk. The floor was tiled in black, white and red to represent a Willys-Knight coupé motoring through a ring of fire. My cousins looked up like they saw a ghost.

"Jim!"

"OK, Harry. Ginger. All right."

"Thought you were —"

"We're back. Just out at Ansley Cemetery. Four Corners."

Harry blanched — went white.

"Want to tell me about it, Harry?"

"Jim, it's a *fortune* —"

"Give 'em money, too?"

Harry looked too terrified to try to lie.

"Five hundred dollars, just to get the ball rolling. Take more later on, of course, when it's a big case with lots of lawyers, but for now —"

"Jesus *Christ!* All yours? Ginger, you put in?"

"I did the digging."

"Night before last?"

Ginger nodded.

Uncle Jim rounded on Harry.

"So you dug up your own grandfather's grave and actually lifted out his *bones?*"

"Weren't you listening? Ginger did the spadework."

"What you do with them?"

Harry scanned the street for customers, but didn't see any.

"Put 'em in a carpetbag, gave 'em to Mr. Bueche. He said they'd prove the Claim. Uncle Jim, I know it *sounds* terrible, but when that skeleton makes us rich, you'll *thank* me."

"*Thank* you, will I? You idiot, how can those bones prove a damn thing? You boys broke the law, and you *will* pay the penalty."

"Yes, sir," said Harry, swallowing hard.

Jail's different from a billion dollars, but I might as well add that Harry and Ginger in fact faced no legal consequences, because when Uncle Jim looked it up he couldn't find any statutes that applied. Maybe it's different now, but my cousins got off scot-free.

"Where'd the Slicks go?"

"New York. Said they'd write."

"Oh, count on it."

Next, the station. The agent in the shack told us the Slicks had taken tickets the previous morning for Clinton, Oklahoma, a junction where several railroads cross. Uncle Jim bought the same for us. Next train was at 8:16 p.m.

Then Gram's. She was sitting, in the parlor with Aunt Effie, shades lowered, both in black dresses, black aprons, black bonnets. I'd not been in there before except to peer at my grandfather's tintype, which still glared from the wall. The furniture, too, was stiff and black.

"Ma."

"Don't worry about *us*, Jim. Life's a vale of tears. Sift it?"

The tibia reposed atop her dining room table, on the runner she wove herself in crazy patterns of red and white. Next to it Uncle Jim deposited his toe bones, buttons and nails like a man putting down the day's pocket change.

"All we could find."

Gram sighed. "Jim, who did it?"

"Don't you worry, Ma. Going after a certain pair of New York Slicks. We'll get Daddy back."

"Been to East View," Gram answered. "Bought four plots: for your Daddy, for Nelly, for me and for— We're moving Nelly." Again I felt someone walk on my grave; still seemed about right. "Bury 'em when you get back."

We ate—Aunt Effie had spent the day in the kitchen—and from the jailhouse Uncle Jim telephoned Castle Fairplay, learning that the posse had dashed off after Frank Holloway's swift palamino precisely an hour after his start.

Also, a reporter from the Vernon *Call* came by to interview Uncle Jim about the body snatching. He couldn't *not* say anything, but kept it short, said he was sorry to hear they thought it rated the front page. Later we saw the story, a stark column about the scene that faced us at the cemetery.

12.

WE WERE STILL STUFFED with roast beef and mince pie when, beneath a streamlined slant of sparks, coupling-rods frantic as a sprinter's elbows, our train came in and carried us off on what I had no doubt was our mission of revenge.

In the course of the three-hour ride to Clinton, Oklahoma, I glimpsed a grand total of five lights or clumps of lights in otherwise pitch-black country; pirate ships we fled on the tossing ocean, or maybe I dreamed that.

At Clinton, Uncle Jim grilled the ticket agent who'd just come on duty. The man got his colleague on the phone at home.

Sure, this fellow told him, he remembered the Slicks — sharp-dressed fellas the day before, right? Headed up to Garden City, Kansas. Probably stay at the Windsor Hotel, *The Waldorf of the Prairies.* Hadn't had to wait long for their train.

We waited hours for ours.

Uncle Jim decided he needed a drink (our family was wet). Someone put him on to an alley doorway across from the station where, after discussing his sheriff's star and *me*, we entered a speakeasy handily converted from a saloon. Over the back bar hung an oil painting of a lady who wasn't wearing clothes — not that she minded. Pink and plump, arms folded behind her head, she was interesting to look at. As he drank his whiskey, Uncle Jim studied her like he was X-raying her skeleton.

Back in the waiting room he said I should get some sleep. Made me nervous, how he sat with legs thrust out, boots occasionally drumming the floor, staring at the wood stove and saying nothing. Vibrating with rage, I was sure.

At last we climbed aboard our train, taking seats on the left-hand side. All night the wind dashed sparks and cinders against the windows from the engine's smoldering fury up ahead. Uncle Jim idly checked over his Colt, not noticing how this made some fellow passengers nervous. It was a fine gun; he'd taught me how to shoot it himself. The trip took four hours, so finally he put the Colt away and, tilting his Stetson over his face, leaned back to get some sleep.

Next thing I knew, he was hauling me to my feet and bumbling me down the aisle and onto a platform that smelled of creosote.

We were in Garden City, Kansas, just able to make out blocky shapes against the star-scattered sky. Across the street stood the Windsor Hotel, rising in brick with a regular rhythm of stone-linteled windows. Great lighted lanterns flanked its corner entrance. We stalked across and went inside.

It was awe-inspiring, something like Castle Fairplay but on an even larger scale: An enormous, oblong, round-cornered lobby rose clear past five tiers of rooms with walnut doors, walnut balustrades and walnut banisters cascading down staircases, red carpet on the floor, at the ceiling a stained-glass skylight, its oily sheen dark against the night. A banner proclaimed *The Waldorf of the Prairies*.

Despite the hour, we got a room—$1.50—on the fourth floor, went to bed and slept the sleep of the dead.

Past lunchtime when we woke up. Running to the window, I saw a town that looked a lot like Vernon. And I thought Wilbarger County was flat? We washed up—in our own bathroom!—and went to find something to eat, but first I put my head over the railing and looked way, way down at the lobby busy with men crossing or stopping to chat with the ladies sitting on the antimacassars. Craned up at the skylight, too, now a crystalline flower garden dripping colors from the sky: *gorgeous.*

We went into the restaurant and, midafternoon though it was, they found food for us. It was a very good hotel, Uncle Jim said; as fine as any in Fort Worth.

"Uncle Jim, how are you going to kill the Slicks?"

This made him laugh.

"Not killing anybody, Bing. Just want Daddy's bones back."

"What if you can't get them?"

He chewed and said nothing.

After eating, we took a turn downtown. I noticed smiles aimed at us on the busy sidewalks, the big out-of-town Sheriff loping intently along, his pint-sized sidekick — sporting a tin star and smaller Stetson — taking giant steps to keep up.

As we went back into the hotel, who should be joshing the clerk at the cigar counter, but Foster Bueche Junior?

"Mr. Bueche," said Uncle Jim behind him.

Bowler hat perched jauntily on the back of his head, liking to hear his name spoken, Junior turned around smiling and, though I detected a flicker in his eyes when he realized who it was, his outward confidence didn't suffer.

"Sheriff. Kid. Out o' your bailiwick, ain't you?"

"Oh, by two states or so, but there's a matter I wish to consult your father about."

"Dad *will* be pleased, but just at the moment I'm afraid he's engaged —"

"Was hoping he'd find time right now."

Their second-floor suite was grand, the sitting room furnished in smart new furniture, bedrooms to either side. As Bueche Junior opened the door, Bueche Senior was seated at the window with the Garden City *Telegram,* one eye squinched shut, doubtless combing it for local heirs to the Edwards Estate.

"Dad—" said his son.

The strain in his voice deflected his father's attention. Senior crumpled the newspaper and came unsteadily to his feet.

"Well, well," he said, bracing himself by grabbing Uncle Jim's hand; even I could see he was *drunk.* "Nice to see you again, Sheriff. Bing. But aren't we out of your jurish—jurish— *jurishdiction?*"

"Matter to discuss," Uncle Jim said.

"By all means," said Mr. Bueche, sitting down abruptly. "Won't you have a seat? Can call for coffee or—care for something stronger—we're friends with a well-connected bellboy."

"Where's my father, Mr. Bueche?" Probably my uncle didn't mean to sound so plaintive.

"Hope you don't think I'm mocking you, Sheriff, if I answer as my dear mother would whenever I asked such a thing: Wherever you left him, sir. Venture to guess somewhere in the soil of Texas?"

"I want his bones, Bueche—the bones you took after violating his grave!"

"Look here, Sheriff, I did no such thing! Would never *do* such a thing!"

"Where are they?"

Bueche & Son were fast thinkers. Looking back, I realize they must have found themselves in similar situations, if perhaps not before faced with a mountain-sized Texas sheriff. I thought it time for Uncle Jim to bring out the Colt—just lay it across his lap as a reminder that he meant business. That's what I would have done.

"Never laid *eyes* on your father's grave, Sheriff, much less *deshecrated* it.

"But I confess bones were given us. A ghastly gift, but

difficult to turn down, you understand. Prefer not to say by whom given. Suffice to shay by persons who, while possibly inshenshi — inshenshi — *inshenshitive* to the *heinoushnessh* of what they were doing, did it with the welfare of their wider family in mind, under the impression that presenting a skeleton in full (but for a leg) would pershuade Trinity Church to give up its real estate.

"Gave us those bones in a carpetbag. Really your father's?"

Now he smiled, as if amused by my cousins' conscientiousness in handing over the genuine article when, bones being bones, *any* would have served.

"In *that* bag," Bueche Junior said, indicating a deflated carpetbag sitting at the wall, adding, as Uncle Jim bounded across the room, making it shake, "Oh, it's *quite* empty now."

Upending it, Uncle Jim bellowed, "Hell you do with them?"

"Father, what *did* we do with them?"

"Didn't we play a game, Foster?" said Bueche Senior. "On the train?"

"That's right, I remember now. Starting at Clinton, Oklahoma?"

"When we realized no one was after us," his father affirmed as Uncle Jim sank into the closest chair as though his legs would support him no longer.

"And played it until we crossed the Arkansas River," his son said.

"I can tell you *exactly* what we did with the bones, Sheriff. Understand, we were feeling good after Vernon — left town richer by $500. Mind you, hoped for more, but $500 is $500! If you're asking for it back—"

"Not asking for it back. Makes for an expensive lesson, but that's the kind people learn from."

"Very wise, sir. In any case, having filled our flasks with remarkably passable Wilbarger whiskey and with, as you'll readily understand, no use for moldy old *bones,* we amused ourselves by rendering them again unto the earth. Decent thing to do, told my son."

"Told *him,* hundred miles of happy dogs," said Junior. "While I could speak."

"What my son means is, at every whistlepost we tossed a bone out the window and took a sip of whiskey."

"And that's a lot of sips!" his son put in.

"And having *shaved* the best for last, and with no wish to test Kansas law in the matter of grave robbery, we tossed the leftovers plus that noble skull (your pappy had a damn big head!) into the Arkansas River from the trestle bridge, sanctifying the act by draining our flasks. Then tried to recover our *shenses* somewhat before arriving here."

Supremely pleased with himself — he was boasting! — Bueche leaned back, holding my uncle's gaze. I wanted to kill them both! And as Uncle Jim glared at the senior Slick, I was sure they were seconds away from getting smashed up *bad.* Only question: Noisy gun or silent fist?

Me? Still would have gone with the Colt.

But Uncle Jim betrayed me! Sat there wilting before my eyes. I could see his anger dissolving, tension leaving his body.

"Come on, Bing," he said finally, getting to his feet. "Let's go talk to the police of this burg, let 'em know what they've got here. Then we've got us a yeggman to catch."

Father and son smiling serenely, without another word my uncle led me out, around the balcony and down the stairs.

The police station was close by, lofting green globe lights over the square. All right, I was thinking, smart to let local law enforcement take over, bring in the Slicks; justice would be served, and I appreciated the professional courtesy involved. But what about *revenge?*

We went in. Uncle Jim identified himself to a uniform

behind a high desk, and asked to speak with his chief.

The chief's office was big and airy with yellowish wainscoting, one whole wall plastered with wanted posters. He welcomed us and listened as Uncle Jim told him about the Slicks and their confidence game, and gave him their names, descriptions and suite number.

"Thanks, Sheriff, we'll keep an eye on 'em," he told us. "Won't get to work their little scheme here."

I burst out, "Tell him about the *bones,* Uncle Jim."

The chief looked interested, but my uncle said, "Not here, Bing, that's a Texas matter."

"And Oklahoma!"

"Well, we're in Kansas. Won't trouble you, Chief—it's personal."

"Gotcha, Sheriff. Staying long?"

"Left my deputies hot on the trail of a bank robber, time I joined them. Frank Holloway, the Oklahoma Yeggman?"

The chief whistled. "He's a bad 'un. Good luck!"

They shook hands, I got a pat on the head—"Pretty lad, ain't you?"—and Uncle Jim led me out.

On the street when he said, "Come on, Bing, let's go check the railroad schedule," I could hold my peace no longer.

"Why didn't you *kill* them, Uncle Jim?"

He took his time answering.

"What good would killing them *do,* Bing, except get us into all kinds of trouble? Retrieve Daddy's bones? Teach them their manners? Believe me, they're not worth it."

"But they *snatched* your father's *body!*"

"Yes, or not them, and I do resent it—and don't appreciate that New York yarn, either—but they're gone from Vernon forever. And think: Would you want to be *them?* Punishment enough."

"Don't you want *revenge,* Uncle Jim?"

"You're young, Bing: 'Course you think you want revenge.

But life's not like *The Count of Monte Cristo*. That's just a children's story. At my age, you'll realize revenge serves no purpose. Trips you up, is all it does."

"But— But— *But—*" And I pummeled him—whaled on him hard as I could, punching his gut over and over, screaming and crying.

People stopped to look, but I couldn't hurt him—he caught my fists and held them in the air, repeating gently, "Simmer down, Bing, simmer down."

My paroxysm lasted—don't know how long. The crying kept on a little; then, deeply disappointed in my uncle, I got ahold of myself and remarked, "I hate you."

"Now, now."

There turned out to be several trains south. Uncle Jim decided on the one at 3:02 a.m.—it seemed an odd choice—and we returned to the Windsor Hotel. From the lobby he was able to telephone Aunt Willie and learn that Rube had just called in from Tucumcari, New Mexico, still on Frank Holloway's trail. After an early supper, we went to bed, leaving word for a 2:30 a.m. knock on the door. They'll do that for a sheriff.

Meanwhile I treated Uncle Jim to silence absolute. Had nothing to say to a coward who'd let go unpunished the outrage of his own father's grave—not to mention lose his nephew's inheritance!

In my silence I considered what *I* should do. As a grandson, not a son, and young at that, my outrage might properly be less than Uncle Jim's, and he might even be right as to the legacy's questionableness. Besides, there were two of them, and I didn't have a gun.

But lying there through the November evening, while Uncle Jim snored softly—having apparently fulfilled *his* full meed of revenge in telling the cops about the Slicks—I realized I couldn't live with myself if I did nothing more. Those Slicks had reached in and filleted me like a fish!

Stealing out of bed, I got dressed in the bathroom, felt Uncle Jim's folded-up clothing for his Colt—but it must have been under his pillow, for I couldn't find it—and went out, closing the door quietly.

I was still so exhausted from the train the night before that things took on an interestingly unreal aspect. Or maybe that came from setting out to do something not like a well-mannered little boy but like a man?

Walking around that balcony, I surveyed the lobby's busy scene, now lighted by electric sconces—it was the lively hour after dinnertime. Going around a second time to screw up my courage, I descended to the lobby.

At the desk I asked for a letter-opener. The clerk registered mild surprise, but handed me a long-bladed one whose enamel handle advertised the hotel. Concealing it in my sleeve, I walked up to the second floor and with a smile on my pretty face knocked at the door of the Bueches' suite.

Kill the son first, I figured. Surprise would help me, and if the elder somehow got away, well, he was pretty far gone, anyway—*pickled.* But I meant to stab both in the heart.

Knocked again, for there was no answer. And knocked ten more times, *loud,* because this was not to be borne!

Possibly still at dinner? Downstairs, I trailed through the dining room, attracting attention despite myself—heard the biddies squeal admiration—but didn't find the Bueches.

At the desk I asked the clerk if he knew where Messrs. Bueche Sr. and Jr. might be?

"Oh, they checked out several hours ago."

"Where'd they go?"

"That I don't know. Called away suddenly, they said."

"Oh," I said, and saw amusement forming on his features as I continued to stand there. Amusement fled when I shook the letter-opener out of my sleeve. "Thanks for this."

"You're welcome," he said.

Furious at being balked of my revenge, I returned to our room, undressed and crept into bed. But I fell asleep surprisingly easily, and slept through until the knock on the door in the middle of the night.

13.

AT THAT HOUR the train was filled with the dead being ferried to Hades.

"Bing, chose this one 'cause it crosses the Arkansas about sunup," Uncle Jim told me in a low voice. "They said one every whistlepost, so we'll get off a stop or two past the river, see what we can find."

"All right, Uncle Jim." Apparently I was speaking to him again.

The windows showed us our own shadowy outlines as we steamed through the night, until I realized I was looking through to fields and woods. The sun was rising as we crossed that trestle bridge over the Arkansas River, and smiling genially when we got off at the little town of Pond Creek, Oklahoma. Over a diner breakfast, Uncle Jim said we were looking for a needle in a haystack, but we'd do our best.

We trekked out of town along the railway. As far as we could see the tracks were laid atop a built-up berm planted with short grass—for our purpose perfect—rising over countryside covered in taller grasses or planted in wheat.

It was slow going, for me especially. Uncle Jim could stride from sleeper to sleeper, but I had to hop from one to the next. He pointed out a weathered concrete post incised *W* as one of the whistleposts the Slicks spoke of. Not knowing where on the train they'd sat, we had to cover both sides of the tracks, and soon discovered that lots of things that look like bones are not in fact bones. We darted down the berm to inspect what turned out to be random pieces of cardboard or steel or, at best, chicken drumsticks. Segments of cattail and some locally prolific cane kept us pouncing in the trackside waste.

After several slow miles we came across a putrefying dog, undoubted bones spilling out of its hide, and some ways on, another whistlepost looming, a single bone, a rib, lying near the berm's bottom. Uncle Jim stooped and reverently picked it up. There was no meat on it and—more brown than white—it looked old, which is why we figured it might be my grandfather's and not the dog's. A slightly stronger flick of the wrist would have landed it eternally beyond recovery in the tall grasses.

Holding it, Uncle Jim climbed back to the rails, collapsed on one, heaved, fought them back—shaking with the effort—then let them come: *Tears,* deluge of *tears.* Crying out miserably, sobs racking him, he wept as I'd never seen a grown man weep.

"It doesn't matter, Uncle Jim," I urged with my arms around him. "Bones are just bones. They get scattered. They're not *him.* Can't matter to *him,* no one can do *him* any harm.

"You've done as much as any son could. Can't sit and cry forever just 'cause it's so sad. You've got to go on living, Uncle Jim."

He clutched me, but his heaves gradually lessened, finally stopped, and he let me go.

"Thanks, Bing. Thanks, little man."

Heaving a mighty sigh, he got to his feet and went down to the bottom of the berm and, squatting, scooped out a hole with that bone.

"You know, Dad was a restless, wandering kind of man," he said. "Born in Alabama, lived all over Texas. No surprise a grave couldn't hold him — *had* to bust out. Looked at one way, it's even *funny*."

He barked something that didn't sound much like a laugh, kissed the rib, placed it in the hole, smoothed dirt over it and stood up.

"Well, think we've done what we can here. No point looking for more, or mentioning it, either. Like you said, doesn't really matter, does it?"

Guessing we were closer to the next stop than the last, we walked on to Kremlin, Oklahoma, ate lunch at another diner and caught the next train.

14.

THE TRAINS FINALLY, gruelingly got us to Tucumcari late the next evening. Checking into the hotel, we found a telegram from Rube saying the posse had reached Wagon Mound, New Mexico. We went to bed.

Unexpectedly, we were the object of attention over breakfast the next morning in the lobby restaurant. We understood why when we saw the Tucumcari *Tomahawk*'s banner headline:

POSSE HOT ON
YEGGMAN'S TRAIL!

As Uncle Jim read, brow furrowed, two men came up and introduced themselves as Mr. Stacy and Mr. Green. Said they were *thrilled* to meet the famous sheriff leading the famous posse going after the famous outlaw, and asked all kinds of questions, including why we were late joining the chase. Uncle Jim, circumspect, mumbled something about other law business.

But Stacy's and Green's excitement struck me as having a hidden point to it. As usual Uncle Jim got there ahead of me.

"So what is it you youngsters do?" he drawled. "Newspaper reporters?"

"No, *sir*," said Stacy and, exchanging a glance with Green, came clean: "Newsreel photographers."

"Pathé News," Green added, handing him a business card.

Blinking, Uncle Jim did not look pleased.

"Thought we might join you," Stacy said, "or trail after. Historic thing, this posse of yours — harks back to the Old West. Deserves to be recorded on film."

"Want to follow, can't stop you," Uncle Jim sighed. "But bear in mind, gentlemen, it's a posse, not a parade. No telling what kinds of country we'll have to get through, what weathers, and the end might be dangerous. Probably will: Frank Holloway's armed and desperate."

"Why we want to be there," said Stacy.

"End of an era, Sheriff," Green said, smacking his lips: "*The last posse.*"

Uncle Jim gave him kind of a funny look.

They had a very good car — a V-8 Cadillac Type 59, in blue — and offered us a lift. Uncle Jim accepted, for the sake of speed, though he regretted the necessity. But I liked being with them; it made me feel important, even if that first day they didn't film anything.

Passing Wagon Mound's gigantic butte that afternoon, we could see in the distance the jagged silhouette of the Sangre de Cristos range. By the time we arrived in Ojo Feliz, where fortunately we found an old inn, the sun was easing itself down the other side via red handholds on the peaks. Thanks to the Cadillac, we were catching up.

Early next morning, knowing the trail would get rougher, we hired five good horses from an old-fashioned livery stable — a big bay for Uncle Jim, a lively gray gelding named Smokey for me, and three chestnuts for Messrs. Stacy & Green and their spare camera and film.

The six dynamic minutes of their finished product — *The Last Posse* — came out just a few weeks later, accompanying the Harold Lloyd feature *Dr. Jack*. It begins with Uncle Jim warily climbing aboard his horse while I jump lightly on mine. As you can tell, I happened to be the more experienced rider.

THE SHERIFF AND HIS LITTLE DEPUTY
MOUNT THEIR STEEDS

That was actually our second mounting; due to some mistake with the lens, Stacy and Green made us get off, go back indoors and come out again.

Then you see us trot out of the village, the street giving way to the unfenced, trackless high desert.

SOME ROUGH COUNTRY, YOU BET!

Well, not too bad. The Cadillac made it without much difficulty. Uncle Jim and I led the cameramen's horses, because it turned out the car was able to keep up along the whole rugged route, making the horses of "the last posse" superfluous (a fact not known to many), except they did pull the Caddy out of deep sand once or twice.

We pressed on all day, going through Guadalupis and over the Charo Pass; Uncle Jim was relentless.

It was tiring to keep that much horseflesh going just with my knees turned in on his sides, but great fun, too. Smokey was a good horse who entered into the spirit of the chase, twitching his ears intelligently, commenting with sweeps of his tail. I liked his horse smell, and the leather squeaks of complaint from saddle and tack; enjoyed being for once more competent than my uncle. Oh, was Uncle Jim sore; back on *terra firma* later on, there was a hitch in his giddy-up for sure.

At the end of the day we at last caught up with my uncle Rube. Funny, really. We saw dust rising ahead, and Uncle Jim remarked that it couldn't be our yeggman, not with that much dust, and he hoped it wasn't our posse, 'cause throwing up that much dust was no way to catch a yeggman, when up we came to find our saddlesore brethren making camp. Their enthusiasm appeared to have worn off considerable. They perked up, though, when Stacy and Green started cranking the camera at them beneath a sunset mess of reds and oranges.

THE SHERIFF JOINS HIS POSSE!

We hobbled the horses to let them feed on the tumbleweeds. Uncle Eustace tried to get us singing after supper, but no one was having it, and we hit the hay around a tumbleweed fire. No creatures troubled us, though Rube's warnings about rattlesnakes and scorpions, and the eyes in the dark he pointed out reflecting the campfire, led the cameramen to bunk in the Cadillac.

At sunrise we were on the move again, amidst a terrific racket of lapwings and — I was surprised — gulls.

THE POSSE KEEPS AT
THE YEGGMAN'S HEELS

Thus far, tracking our outlaw had required no special expertise: We just followed his tire tracks and hoofprints, clear enough on dirt trails and becoming steadily fresher and better defined as he gradually ascended the desert scrub. But now, the ground getting rocky, it became more like you used to read about or see in the movies. Taking his pony over the hardest ground, Frank Holloway *vanished*. I lost the trail.

But Uncle Jim didn't. In that beautiful, lonesome country he had to glean it from the subtlest signs; for instance, tilting his head, he could somehow discern hoof-sized flattened areas of pebble. How, I don't know, but glean it he did. His brothers followed in perfect faith, but some of the other deputies began grumbling that we were lost and getting more so.

I wondered why one man on a fast pony hadn't left us in his dust, but Uncle Jim explained the pressure of having a posse after you; said he'd never heard of anyone chased by one who wasn't caught in the end if only the chasers kept at it.

THE SHERIFF DECIDES THE ROUTE

Sun high overhead, when not even he could see traces of our prey, Uncle Jim brought us to a halt and addressed us. Normally phlegmatic and the opposite of showy, in that scene he looks positively gesticulatory; probably part of what he told me was the hardest part of being sheriff — getting people to do what he wanted.

"S'got choices," he now announced, "so we have to outguess our man." Pointing due west and northwest, he said, "Could take either of those passes. But I suspect he's headed to *Sheepdip.*" He indicated a higher pass to the southwest. "Went through years ago, Rube and me. Little village, but up above's an old adobe strong as a castle."

Uncle Jim told us that from that adobe one man could command the whole pass, and he suspected Frank Holloway, if he got there, would dig in and try to stave us off — said that's what he'd do. And if he couldn't stave us off, might be able to slip past in the dark.

"So that's my guess. Let's try and make Sheepdip tonight."

Then comes my close-up, squinting past the lens with an exact if unconscious imitation of Uncle Jim's expression. (People at the showing I saw laughed.)

We headed up foothills of the Sangre de Cristos towards the ancient village that was our goal. The track got steeper. The falling sun lighted tumbleweeds from beneath, cupping them like green candles. Pathé thought it was cactus.

ROUGH GOING THROUGH
THAT CACTUS!

15.

BEFORE SUNSET WE REACHED the old village known in English (not that anyone there spoke it) as Sheepdip. It consisted of a church and a dozen adobe houses—more a Mexican village than an American one. Sure enough, the hill above was crowned by an adobe still bright in the sun, and though we couldn't see Frank Holloway, the villagers confirmed by signs that he'd gone up there a short time before, after almost buying out the only store.

Helped by the village priest, Uncle Jim saw to the night's arrangements. While we ate the chicken and beans the villagers kindly sold us, and laid out our bedrolls in an empty house, no one paid the Pathé crew any mind, and Stacy & Green—sensing that more exciting camera angles lay above—abruptly drove straight up the steep track to the yeggman's eyrie.

Foolhardy, but luckily he didn't shoot them.

When Rube realized what they'd done—the supplies in that Cadillac could sustain an army—he was so upset he stamped on his hat. But Uncle Jim stayed calm.

"Interesting narrative twist," was all he said. "Hope they keep out of the line of fire."

The newsreel shows what they found at the top of the hill.

HERE HE IS AT LAST:

THE OKLAHOMA YEGGMAN!

Doubtless mindful of his Hollywood ambitions, Frank Holloway affably greets Pathé to his lair, pulling at his mustache in close-up and managing to resemble Douglas Fairbanks: composed, thoughtful, artistic, handsome. In compelling profile he peers out a window at his palomino, and behind him you can see a water barrel and heaped-up bags of beans and canned goods.

OUGHT TO BE IN PICTURES, RIGHT, LADIES?

WELL, HE'S HEADED FOR HOLLYWOOD!

Even on film he gave me the willies.

Uncle Jim dispatched teams of deputies further along the base of the hill, out of sight of the village, with food and bedrolls and instructions to watch out for Frank Holloway sneaking past, and orders to shoot if he tried it.

NIGHT FALLS OVER THE VILLAGE

As I went to sleep I heard Uncle Jim telling Rube, "Afraid he'd find that roost. 'Less we want to be here all winter, need some kind of ruse. Head-on assault won't work."

The next day was endless, boring and futile. Uncle Jim organized an attack and, as he predicted, it failed. He and Rube showed themselves so as to draw Frank Holloway's fire while deputies tried to sneak up the hill's backside. But the legendary gunman was no dupe, and the deputies had to retreat. There was no rousting him. Uncle Jim said we were embarked on an old-fashioned siege and he didn't know how long it might last.

At sunrise the next morning when I drew up my knees and rubbed the sleep from my eyes, Uncle Rube was staring at me from across the room. It was unnerving. Over coffee and *huervo rancheros* he did more of it. Finally he went over and conferred with Uncle Jim. Plain to see Rube had an idea and, from the way he kept nodding my way, plain it concerned *me*; plain also that Uncle Jim resisted.

But Rube kept at it. Speaking confidentially to Uncle Jim, he pointed up the hill, at the sun and at me; pointed to everybody eating breakfast, back at the way we'd come, and again at *me*.

Uncle Jim looked at me, too—speculatively, fingers worrying his chin. Rube persisted until at last Uncle Jim shrugged and his stance lost its quality of resistance.

They disappeared. Fine by me—they were making me nervous.

Soon they reappeared.

"Bing, we've come up with a plan," Uncle Jim told me. "But depends on *you*. Don't like it, say so. Never ask you to do something you don't want to do."

"I'll do it, Uncle Jim. What is it?"

What could it be but that they wanted their brave nephew to sneak up the hill and take the Oklahoma Yeggman? Be the big hero? I was all for it!

Rube spoke up. "Bing, think you could hold a gun on Frank Holloway while the rest of us run up there? Shoot him if you had to?"

"Sure I could," I scoffed. Why was he even asking?

"Now, he knows you," said Uncle Jim, "so we need to disguise you. Knew it was you, doubt he'd shoot, but he *might*, and anyway he'd know something's up."

"Good idea."

"Sure you can shoot *him* before he shoots you?"

"Said so, didn't I?"

"Only if you have to," Uncle Jim cautioned. "But good. OK then, put this on."

At his nod a village mother and daughter came over giggling. Over the mother's arm was draped a bright blue embroidered *dress*—obviously a costume of her slender daughter's. The girl carried a shawl.

Chills went down my spine.

In that era, every male in the country carried deep inside him, in a place seldom visited, the suppressed memory of wearing dresses. It's what they used to put little boys in. Boys wore dresses—*and* long hair, and ribbons, too—until they started walking, *and* afterwards. Mothers loved having their sons in dresses, and sons do love their mothers. I'm not sure I or my compeers got into short pants until we started school. (As for myself, I arrived at Vernon still in short pants; when I stepped off the train, Uncle Jim took one look and even before bringing me to the jail dragged me to Craig & Son's, and now I wore denim like most every man in Texas.)

Inside I quailed; but after declaring I'd go up that hill by myself, how would it look to cavil and refuse? Besides, my hero Huck Finn wore a dress that memorable day he gave away that he was a boy by clapping his knees together when the old lady tossed that knot of lead to him. Surely I was smarter than Huck Finn?

Floating the dress over me, mother and daughter let it fall, the girl looping my neck with beaded necklaces while the woman, clucking in admiration (turns out the Spanish for *aww!* is pretty darn close to the English), brushed my curls and folded them beneath that shawl, and couldn't resist pinching my cheek. In my right hand Uncle Jim—saying to keep hold of it but out of sight under the shawl—placed his personal Colt. For my left hand Rube proffered a pail filled with peaches from someone's cold storage.

"See, coming up to welcome him to Sheepdip," Rube explained.

"*La Estrellita*," said the mother. "*Nuestro pueblo.*"

"Pail in the left hand, right hand on the gun," Uncle Jim added, "else pulls the dress off balance."

"All right, all right."

"*Que bonita!*" murmured the daughter.

"Do look purty at that, nephew," Rube sniggered. "But you're safe, he'd never fire on a girl."

"Do it myself if I could," Uncle Jim said, flashing a smile. "But it wouldn't work."

I was just grateful no one spelled out how my pretty face inspired the whole idea.

"When he comes out for the peaches, put the gun on him," Uncle Jim said. "My rifle will be on him while Rube and everyone runs up. He'll be in my sights at all times, Bing, and if he menaces you I won't hesitate to shoot him."

"OK, Uncle Jim," I said casually. In actuality I felt more nervous than I cared to let on.

"Ready?"

"*Yes,*" I said with irritation, and went outdoors and started uphill with that pail. Didn't try to walk like a girl with that silly *this hip, that hip* wobble, just labored up the track in the sunshine.

WHO'S *THIS* LOVELY SEÑORITA?

At first I didn't look to see if Frank Holloway was watching me. The newsreel shows that he was, suspiciously. Then I figured if I really were some girl bringing him peaches, I *would* look at him, so I start glancing over, and you can see him relax.

He even comes out into the open, rifle in hand but held towards the ground. On film it looks flirtatious; can't help that. The actual sight of him was unnerving. Hellfire burned behind those snake's eyes, and I worried that he or the Pathé crew might recognize me, and then what would happen?

So what *did* happen? My bladder commanded me to pee — to pee that *instant!*

Should have done it down below, but it wasn't an issue then. Now the urgency was *agony!*

UH-OH, NATURE CALLS!

Terrified of peeing myself, I put down the basket — keeping hold of the gun, however — turned aside, hitched up my skirts and relieved myself as I watched a thunderstorm stiltwalk across the Panhandle a hundred miles away: *Ahhh.*

HEY, THAT'S NO *SEÑORITA!*

Hearing distant yells as I buttoned up, I turned my head to see Frank Holloway, features *murderous*, raising that rifle, then saw his feet fall out from under him — actually saw the heel fly off his boot, heard the shot that did it and his yelp — and watched him topple to the ground, gun flying some distance away.

Raised my Colt to stop him from drawing his pistols or scrabbling over to recover the rifle.

CAREFUL, FRANK!

The newsreel shows him getting up and, hands in the air, wobbling straight at me — they were terribly high heels, with one gone he was way off balance — but of course it doesn't show what he said to me, which was, "Kid, let me go, thousand bucks in it for you."

Did I waver? No.

"No."

"*Two* thousand, kid — in *gold.*"

"*No!*"

He sneered, "Anyway, sure do make one helluva pretty gal!"

I pulled the trigger and shot Frank Holloway.

The yeggman hit the ground, wallowed there groaning. Didn't know how bad I might have hurt him, nor did I care. The rude thing I said to him came out treble. My voice wasn't my own in those days, but this was the final occasion on which I recall speaking as a boy soprano.

GOOD WORK, LASSIE!
UM—*LADDIE!*

The deputies meanwhile ran up the hill and took him. Last of all came Uncle Jim, lumbering up with his bone-sighted Winchester.

"Good job, Bing," he said. "You OK?"

"Fine." Thank God it came out low and crusty. "What a shot, Uncle Jim!"

"Wasn't aiming for his *heel.*"

Rube taunted, "Hey, Frank, caught you flat-footed!"

The newsreel's last frames show Frank Holloway snarling in handcuffs and no hat, left sleeve dark with a spreading stain, at his feet a Gladstone bag spilling over with bank loot.

OH-OH, NO HOLLYWOOD
FOR HOLLOWAY!
LOOKS LIKE PRISON INSTEAD!

16.

STACY AND GREEN merely shouted their goodbyes before driving off like bats out of Hell. Must have made good time, too, wherever they were headed, to get their newsreel into theatres as fast as they did.

We got going ourselves, though slowed up some by Uncle Jim's insistence that Frank Holloway be cuffed either to himself or Rube day and night.

Next morning as Uncle Jim boiled his coffee on the campfire, I heard him say, "Rube, I'm quitting. This is it, I quit."

"*Quitting?*"

"Frank Holloway, that's business as usual. But losing *Daddy?*" He shook his head. "Job's yours, you want it. Election next year, but that's nothing to be afraid of."

They shut up then, realizing the yeggman on Rube's wrist was waking up. Maybe they realized I was watching, too.

Frank Holloway tossed a gibe first thing.

"Lucky shot, Jim. Aiming at what, my *head? Heart?* And get the heel of my *boot?* Shouldn't let you anywhere *near* a gun."

"Now, now, Frank."

"And your nephew—niece?—*nephew:* What a vicious kid! Didn't have to *shoot* me! Newsreel'll prove it, and when my jury comes in not guilty, I intend to sue. Then it's off to Hollywood, while you and your niece—*nephew?*—are stuck in that hole."

"Vernon's no hole, Frank."

"Not exactly New York, is it? Your false-teeth pals reeled you in hook, line and sinker, didn't they? Got your money *and* your daddy's bones. Been laughing about that ever since, believe me.

"And something about your nephew you *don't* know, Jim: He was in on—"

"Shut up!" I shouted. "SHUT UP, FRANK HOLLOWAY!"

The yeggman smiled a crafty little smile as I grabbed Uncle Jim and led him apart.

"Uncle Jim, I knew about the Groves Claim sooner than I let on," I confessed, "but not about the bodysnatching, I swear."

Oh God. Looked at me like he couldn't believe it, as if I'd buffeted first one cheek and then the other.

"Knew about the *Claim*, Bing? Told me earlier, maybe we could have run the Slicks out of town before anyone did any digging."

He walked off. Frank Holloway smirked as I followed.

After about a hundred paces my uncle rounded on me.

"Well, Bing, I'm disappointed."

"I'm sorry, Uncle Jim."

"Don't you see: Believing in magic—that you're somehow the heir to millions of dollars—is akin to Frank Holloway's way of looking at things? You want it, so you deserve it, you with Manhattan Island, him with his bank hauls? *You* feel entitled, *he* feels entitled, it's a great big mess." Looking to see how I took this, he added, "But I'm glad you told me."

"Glad you told *me,* Uncle Jim." We shook hands.

After we dropped off the livery horses at Ojo Feliz—that Smokey was a good one and I hated to say goodbye—I rode the palomino all the way back to Castle Fairplay.

"Something to bear in mind about the Duke, Bing," said Uncle Jim as we rode into the forecourt at last. "Life's hard for everybody—no exceptions. Remember that, life's just *hard.*"

"Yes, Uncle Jim."

To celebratory bagpipes, we walked up the steps and entered the hall, where pinyon pine crackled in the fireplaces. The Duke was happy to see us, glad his horses were home and in good health—well exercised, for sure—and *delighted* we had our prisoner. This time he enforced no freedom-of-the-castle nonsense regarding the yeggman, but forthrightly suggested putting him in the dungeon.

"You've got a *dungeon?*"

"Castle, isn't it? This way."

We followed him down to the cellars, where there *was* a dungeon—rock-walled cells stacked with crates of illicit liquor (Uncle Jim took no notice). A cell was emptied out, fresh straw brought and Rube cuffed Frank Holloway to an iron ring in the floor.

"He'll be fine," said the Duke. "Sorry, Frank, but I can't interfere."

"M'lud, you don't have to do this— Duke! *Duke!*"

The door shutting on him was a relief, though frankly I was afraid Frank Holloway would manage to ignite his straw with a hellfire glance and burn down the whole Castle, us with it.

The bank loot went into the Duke's safe overnight.

Relaxing over whiskey, ignoring the interruptions his excited deputies every minute offered, Uncle Jim recounted to the Duke how we chased and captured the Oklahoma Yeggman. I shifted uncomfortably when he got to my part. Didn't take it easy on me: Described in detail my ensemble, the dress's fabric, ornamentation and fit—Rube supplementing some points, disputing others—and everyone chimed in how fetching it looked on me. Eyes shining, the Duke sighed.

Then, hearing about how I stopped to pee, he almost had a fit laughing.

Next morning Rube freed the ripe-smelling Frank Holloway from the dungeon and cuffed him to his wrist. We left, the Duke shaking the men's hands, but hugging me close, kissing my cheek and inviting me to visit any time, stay long as I liked.

We hauled our prisoner the rest of the way in the backseat of a Willys-Knight. By the time our four crowded autos reached Vernon, other cars were following behind us, honking: *A-OO-gah! A-OO-gah!*

We lined up in front of the jail as townspeople flocked to welcome us home and inspect our haul, Frank Holloway snarling like a bear on a chain. We posed for a homecoming photograph, too, but that photo's not on display anywhere I can find. As I recall, people criticized it for showing our posse dusty and exhausted while the Oklahoma Yeggman summoned his showman instincts to pose smiling and victorious, his free hand raised in a fist.

"You'd be the star at your own hanging," Uncle Jim remarked as we brought him inside.

Aunt Willie greeted us at the door. She looked terribly sad, which was jarring. Soon as Uncle Jim had his prisoner safely in an end cell next to an empty one—doubting out loud that bond would be offered this time—she took him aside.

Whatever she told Uncle Jim made him sad, too, and he turned to look at me. But if he had anything to tell me, he didn't say it then. Couldn't, for the editor of the Vernon *Call* came by and insisted on wringing a full account from us.

Adjourning to the Swasteeka, we told him our story over steak (Uncle Jim glossing over my contribution, thank goodness), in between people dropping by to congratulate us. The Mayor showed up and made a speech impromptu.

After we returned to the jail, the worst thing that's ever happened to me happened. Uncle Jim had me brush my teeth and get in my pajamas, and you can believe I was looking forward to sleeping in my own bed at last. But he came in and sat down on it, something he never did.

"Bing, have some bad news for you. Your Ma's been ill."

"I know it."

"Very ill. She had a cancer. It got worse and— Well, day before yesterday she died. Don't know how to tell you but straight out."

I was outraged! Furious that Uncle Jim had treasured up this morsel over dinner and kept it from me! Madder still at never having a chance to say goodbye!

Of course, even I could vaguely see how unfair my tantrum was to a man himself mourning his baby sister. Seems her illness—cancer of the breast—was why they sent me to Texas in the first place. No one told me anything.

Now I could stay or go home, my choice.

"Going home *tomorrow*. Won't stay *here*, you can bet on that!"

"Well, your Dad's bringing her back to bury. Be here in a few days. Can leave with him, you want."

17.

MET THE TRAIN Friday, at the end of the day when sunset was blunting the arrow-headed shadows. Dad, a slender figure in black, greeted Uncle Jim gravely after flicking a surprisingly disinterested glance over his own son. Then he turned and startled.

"*Bing!* My word, son, didn't recognize you! You've grown up!"

Partly my haircut. Dawdy's Barber Shop had cut off the curls my Ma loved.

We watched a coffin being unloaded from the baggage car onto an iron-wheeled cart under the emollient eyes of Mr. Drew, the undertaker. The funeral was to be Monday morning at the ME church, burial to follow.

Ma always said Dad liked her brothers, and back at the jailhouse he did seem glad to see them again. But he didn't attend too closely to our accounts of our big adventure. Though bringing in the Oklahoma Yeggman was still the talk of the town and stuff of daily headlines in the *Call,* Dad's interest seemed forced. I offered to introduce him to the outlaw himself, just downstairs, and he said, no, thanks, that was all right.

Uncle Jim fed us at the Swasteeka, and next day drove us out to the old Beaver Creek spread, which held some talismanic value to the family, even if it was now just weathered timbers on

Waggoner land. We squinted at the derrick a half mile off where, drilling for water for their cattle, the Waggoners by accident had lately struck oil. This time we skirted the old cemetery. The broken marker and Nelly's stone pillow had been taken up and carried to East View. Nelly's remains also had been exhumed. It was to be a triple funeral — though of course she and my grandfather had had theirs already — and joint burial.

Monday morning, family and friends gathered at Gram's for my grandfather's inurnment. That was a new word to me. Ma's coffin was there, too, in the parlor with Nelly's little new one. Both stayed closed, to my relief, though there was an undertone of disappointment among visitors.

Gram wore a white dress and bonnet to match, its flaps untied and ribbons hanging. However ancient she was, today her wrinkles were smooth, her face tight. Scandalized, Aunt Effie assured us she'd laid out a black dress, but that Gram rejected it.

Out in the sunny back yard, Mr. Drew presented what he called his finest glazed-porcelain urn as a repository for my grandfather's shinbone, handing it to Gram in her rocking chair and receding from her presence. Standing against the fence, Harry and Ginger watched shamefacedly. I wondered whether Gram knew it was two of her own grandsons who snatched her husband's body. She'd accepted Uncle Jim's apology for coming home without his bones, saying he'd done his best.

The urn was very nice, only too small. Gram reached for the tibia reposing beside her on the picnic table, unscrewed the urn's figured brass top and put it in. A third or more of it poked out. I guessed that Mr. Drew's joiner was about to get a lightning commission for another box.

But Gram pulled at Uncle Clois's shoulder, he bent double to hear, nodded and hastened indoors.

When he came out he handed her a hacksaw and she got to

her feet. Chatter ceased. I think this demonstration of pioneer practicality surprised us, but no one interfered as Gram pinched the bone where its length stuck out of the urn, then put it against the table's edge and preliminarily ran the blade across it. I stopped breathing as the saw rasped back and forth. A cloud of white smoke — no, bone dust — rose up and I think I expected an explosion. I will never forget the sight nor, seconds later, the snap.

Gram tenderly weighed the pieces and stuffed them into the urn. Dropping in also those toe bones — with the sound of pennies deposited in a piggy bank — she clapped on the lid. Now I saw tears washing her cheeks, though no sound emerged.

But *I* burst into *howls* of grief! I was ashamed, but couldn't help it! Uncle Jim turned and hugged me close, murmuring, "It's OK, Bing, it's OK." Ten different women delightedly declared, "The boy misses his mommy!" Uncle Jim just kept saying, "It's OK, Bing, it's OK."

The funerals came right after the inurnment. Mr. Drew's custom, famous in the region, was to carry his customers to their graves in an ox cart: He owned two blindingly white oxen the size of buffalo. Ma's brothers loaded her coffin and Nelly's, stood their father's urn between them, and the oxen pulled the cart to the Methodist-Episcopal Church with the rest of us walking behind it. Keeping my hand on Ma's coffin, I felt the power of those oxen transmitted to my arm as their feet dug ahead.

The minister had a field day. He took pains to emphasize how, at the Last Judgment, resurrection awaits bodies represented by as little as a sliver of bone. Hearing that, Gram visibly relaxed; it addressed her chief concern, that losing all of her husband but a tibia would deprive her of eternity with him. Now she was reassured. He praised my grandfather as a pioneer of Wilbarger County, Nelly as one cut down too soon, and Ma as a daughter of Wilbarger come home at last.

Then they loaded the oxcart for the journey to East View and the newly-purchased plots on the slope beneath a sky of coconut macaroons. There everything was properly committed to the ground, over more words from the minister: Ma's coffin lowered, and Nelly's, and my grandfather's urn laid in its special hole beneath his relocated, patched-up and steel-braced monument.

We moved a little away as Ginger took off his coat and he and the gravedigger, his old boss, partially filled in the graves. Then, having the grace to look embarrassed, he helped his men push a cement mixer near. His excavation business had this concrete-pouring offshoot, so they knew what to do. They shoveled cement and water into the mixer and turned it and turned it, and through a trough poured it into the graves, then made another batch, and another. Gram refused to leave even as some began drifting towards her house for lunch.

Bothered by that concrete, I left while the mixer still turned.

Aunt Willie's insistence on overseeing lunch gave me an anticipatory stomachache. But to my surprise, the food was ample and good: potato salad tangy, deviled eggs delicious, liverwurst sandwiches beyond reproach. Whatever the prisoners had to put up with that day, Aunt Wilhelmina's husband's kinfolk dined well; she stuffed us speechless.

But Gram was understandably maudlin. She went around repeating, "Buried my husband twice now, won't be long for me." (Nor was it; only months later she succumbed peacefully to her kidney complaint, entirely ready to go.)

Uncle Jim saw Dad and me onto the train the next day.

"Been a lifesaver, Bing," he said. "Come back any time."

18.

BACK HOME in Pasadena I saw the newsreel and the Harold Lloyd movie that followed. Fortunately, no one appeared to recognize me onscreen, and I volunteered nothing, so no one made me the butt of their jokes or teased me about being the boy in the dress; conversely, no one knew I was a hero. My feelings were mixed.

After New Year's I started the new semester at my old school. Of course I was sorry to miss Frank Holloway's trial, but Uncle Jim wrote me about it and sent clippings.

Judge Ohlmacher sat a jury of Vernon folk pleased to be diverted from their ordinary occupations. Despite his stay in jail—this time fed by Aunt Willie—Frank Holloway apparently looked dashing, hair and mustache black, trig in a new black suit. A hint of a slight strain on the pearl buttons at his belly was, to Uncle Jim's critical eye, the only element at odds with the figure the yeggman sought to portray of that ever-popular Western figure, the compleat outlaw.

His city-slicker lawyer arrived in his yellow Pierce-Arrow, but didn't do him much good. Judge Ohlmacher pushed the witnesses along briskly, and by lunchtime had elicited eyewitness testimony about both Harrold bank robberies, including firm identifications of Frank Holloway.

It was very efficient. The jury, hearing a teller recite how the bank robber's Colt scared her into contemplating eternity, turned to assess the yeggman's sneer. Of course, Frank Holloway sneered; he repelled all charges with a sneer, for he was someone who got away with such things. If not him, who?

Uncle Jim's and Rube's testimony closed the trial's first day. In flat, persuasive terms they described responding to both robberies and, after the second one, the posse's chase. The jury listened and believed.

Fortunately, I wasn't subpoenaed to testify about walking up that hill in the guise of a *señorita,* and Uncle Jim assured me my role was referred to only indirectly.

The next morning, the yeggman declined to testify in his own defense. His lawyer instead attacked the bank teller's eyesight and introduced a thin parade of character witnesses. Meanwhile the men in the jury box sat with legs jiggling impatiently, shoulders squared as though to say, *"Let's get this over with."*

At noon they retired to a jury-room lunch catered by the Swasteeka, and afterwards shuffled burping back into the courtroom, a good taste in their mouths, to pronounce Frank Holloway guilty on both counts. Judge Ohlmacher thanked them and sentenced the yeggman to seven years in prison, and the next day two Texas Rangers carried him off to work the cotton fields at Huntsville Penitentiary.

UNCLE JIM LATER told me the denouement. Frank Holloway served his time – his hard time. Came out gaunt and gray and, returning to his old stomping grounds, fell in with old friends in Tulsa.

Not a week after his release, those friends were dredging up some ancient resentment. Rumor had it that it concerned the division of loot from that British Columbia bank job. In a flourish of pure poetry, they took him one night a little ways out of town, to Gunfighter's Hill, and there made him dig a shallow grave, sit down in it and take in the back of his head the bullet that at last ended the career of the Oklahoma Yeggman.

Uncle Jim's law enforcement career closed way earlier, hard on Frank Holloway's conviction. Having informed the Commissioners, the Mayor, the Vernon *Call* and Aunt Wilhelmina, he resigned as Sheriff of Wilbarger County and moved to the little ranch he'd worked part-time for years, northeast of town near the Red River, and became the cattleman he always wanted to be; although it wasn't too much later that his prosperous brother Eustace lured him to become his partner in the new *Groves Bros. Oil Co.*

The Commissioners summoned Rube and, after frank discussion of his admitted inability to shoot anyone, appointed him Sheriff until the election. As Rube was unmarried, the arrangement whereby Aunt Willie cooked for the prisoners continued, so she never moved out of the jail. Rube moved in but continued to take his meals at the Swasteeka (which after Pearl Harbor became the Wilbarger Grille). He won the next election, never even having to announce, he was so popular, and in fact was Sheriff for many years before being succeeded by a nephew; a family concern indeed.

Fortunately no occasion ever arose that called for Rube to shoot anyone.

II. That's My Story

The Oil King spent $50,000 a year buying athletes for USC under false pretenses. The faculty permitted these husky lumbermen and ranch hands to pass farcical exams — any professor who flunked a quarterback would be looking for another job. Didn't the Oil King show what he thought of professors by paying a football coach *three times* the salary of the best?

Along with turning college athletics into a swindle came underworld accompaniments — bootleggers, bookmakers and prostitutes. The purpose was to win games, the reward *$200,000* in gate receipts. Of this the whole student body was proud, made one by *college spirit*.

— Upton Sinclair
Oil
(*adapted*)

Whatsisname, on the road to Damascus.

— William Kennedy
Legs

1.

"JUST SEE THE LITTLE MAN STRUT!" murmured my boss in awe. "Richest man in California!"

"He looks like the Monopoly man," I said.

Mr. Thomas laughed, because it was true. The codger coming towards us, lifting his knees high, resembled the board-game mascot in every detail: He had the top hat, the brushy white mustache, the morning suit, the gold watch-chain across his plump belly, patent leather shoes and *spats*. A jewel topped his walking stick, and into his right eye was screwed a *monocle*. That monocle marked the only difference between the Monopoly man on the game box, game board, game cards and Mr. Andrew Cassidy, the richest man in California.

His cars had just arrived at the Dome, in the lead a pair of motorcycles mounted by men in leather uniforms and leather helmets, followed by a gleaming black Packard V-12 limousine—a custom job with wonderful lines—and, bringing up the rear, a black Packard sedan. Four bulky men in dark suits piled out of the sedan and, doing a kind of marching-band number, took their places, two flanking the limousine's door, facing each other, and two at the Dome's entrance, hands held loosely at their sides, eyes flicking around the empty sidewalk. *Bodyguards. Gunmen.*

Waiting in his car was a blonde woman swaddled in furs—

furs, in *September,* in *Los Angeles.* Not that she wasn't gorgeous, but there was something a little hardened to her, something *varnished.* I expected she was his daughter or granddaughter. After retouching her lips, she put down her compact and blew me a kiss.

Gaping, I turned to find Mr. Delbert scowling past me. He nudged me to open the door.

I pushed it open and the tycoon entered with a sidewise glance at me: *"Someone I should know? I think not."* The monocle made his watery eye enormous, but instead of the Monopoly man's well of benevolence, it was an aperture to hellfire.

"Good morning, Mr. Cassidy," said Mr. Thomas. "Would Mrs. Cassidy care to come inside where it's cooler?"

"Good morning, good morning. No, thank you, Mr. Raven, my wife's fine where she is. I'm just here to— Well, you know why I'm here."

"Indeed," said Thomas Raven.

"Always liked this room," Cassidy remarked, waving his stick about. "Now, where's your brother?"

"Right here, Mr. Cassidy," said Delbert Raven.

The Dome was the Raven brothers' Westwood Village headquarters—HQ, sales office, monument to their company and their aspirations. From the outside it resembled a baroque church, but indoors was like a bank—a thick-walled structure topped by a towering dome over a terrazzo-floored rotunda, offices tucked in behind. The dome's underside was frescoed in signs of the zodiac, and from it hung electroliers enameled in blue and gold, the colors of the neighboring University of California at Los Angeles; every streetlight in Westwood was similarly enameled blue and gold. Mine was one of the desks in the rotunda, among easels displaying renderings and maps.

Mr. Thomas making to escort him to his office, Cassidy said, "No, no, can do this right here," and slipped a silk-gloved hand into his jacket's breast pocket with that shirring sound of silk touching silk. "Just wanted to hand-deliver this month's cheque from the Caldego Oil Company: $8,781. Smidgeon less than last month, but not too shabby, eh?"

The Monopoly man beamed as Mr. Thomas lavished admiration on the cheque. Mr. Delbert looked less joyful.

"Thank you, Mr. Cassidy," said Mr. Thomas. "Good of you to bring it by."

"Happy to. So how're your Bruins coming along?" The magnified eye flashed. "Bought yourself any ringers yet?"

"No, have you?" countered Mr. Delbert.

"Team's in championship form this year," Mr. Thomas assured him. "Lots of great kids coming up."

"Glad to hear it. After your last season? And the one before that, and— Well, they'll have their work cut out with my Trojans. When's that game?"

"October 26," said Mr. Delbert. "UCLA *versus* USC, Los Angeles Memorial Coliseum."

"October 26," echoed Cassidy. "First time in three years, eh? Destined to be a great gridiron rivalry, mark my words. Gentlemen care to make a wager?"

"Certainly," they said at the same moment. The brothers weren't twins—Mr. Delbert was 18 months older than Mr. Thomas—but they looked a lot alike, lived next door to each other, were both divorced, and when you worked for them you realized they thought alike, too.

"Capital," said Cassidy. "Let's keep it—what's that word my wife likes?—let's keep it *prudent*. How about ten shares of Caldego Oil, $1 par value per share. That too rich for you?"

The Ravens looked at each other. It seemed to me they liked what they heard, but didn't want to show it.

"All right," said Mr. Delbert. "You're on."

And they shook hands, the brothers managing to look grim

while Cassidy chortled.

"Cheer up, gentlemen," he said. "You haven't lost yet. Probably you're too sharp for an old man like me, but I never could resist a little bet. Anything to encourage the youngsters."

Cassidy was the University of Southern California's biggest booster, as the Ravens were of UCLA. He'd lately donated USC's campus crown jewel, Cassidy Memorial Library, in honor of his dead only son. It cost him more than a million dollars. The Ravens, of course, had sold the State the site for UCLA's campus for a cool two million under market value, intending Westwood Village—their development abutting it that they liked to proclaim *The Second Hollywood*—to prosper from its proximity. However, it being 1935, not much was happening. Hence, keeping the bet to ten bucks seemed to me, too, to be prudent.

With more shirring of silk, Cassidy's hand delved back into his breast pocket.

"I give you your cheque?"

"You did, Mr. Cassidy. Thank you."

"Wife says my memory's one minute long these days. Well, then, gentlemen, until next month. And see you at the game, too: Troy *versus* Bruins, Coliseum, on— What's that date?"

"October 26, Mr. Cassidy. See you there."

Knees high, humming a merry tune, stick tapping the pavement at every step, the Monopoly man toddled back to his limousine in another spectacle of bodyguards falling in behind and chauffeur opening the door to his discontented-looking wife.

The motorcycle escorts kicked their engines into thunder and the procession drove off up Westwood Boulevard.

AN EXCITING FIVE MINUTES, to have the richest man in the state with us, but after he was gone, and the office boy sent running to the bank, the Dome settled down to its usual torpor.

The Raven brothers had multifarious interests, but the sales office, where I was in my third week of work, was where they sold — *tried* to sell — lots and houses in Westwood. The Dome and its few neighbors poked up out of mostly bare hills and flats like a frontier town — well, a frontier town with a 170-foot tower rising over its Fox Theatre, and palms being planted along the boulevards.

I sat down at my desk and shared a smile with my colleague Doreen at hers. That the Dome looked and felt like a bank, Mr. Delbert told me, was meant to convey solidity and trustworthiness to people who, we hoped, would pay thousands for lots that, at the moment, hosted nothing more than a few untroubled lizards. I'd heard the brothers declare that the Depression didn't trouble them, that the future of Los Angeles real estate, which they owned so much of, was as glittering as ever. But that didn't prevent us who worked for them from observing that things were tight and getting tighter.

Oh, was selling those lots slow going.

But after a malted-milk lunch across the street at Crawford Drugs, I was pleased to see returning to the Dome a couple I'd met the day before, Mr. and Mrs. Willard, he a shoe-store owner who told me his wife deserved a nice new home.

I'd pulled out the maps, the plats, the blueprints and floor plans, interrogated Mrs. Willard as to her tastes and preferences, discussed down payments, mortgages, interest rates and contractors, run them uphill in the office Essex on newly-paved streets, led them through two model homes, and conducted them over the scrub to an overlook where, I told them, they might build, say, a four-bedroom, two-bath Spanish Mission-style house with a view taking in the whole Los Angeles Basin. Sweeping my arm from the just-opened Griffith Observatory past Downtown, Catalina Island, Beverly Hills, Santa Monica and Malibu, I quoted a price of $15,000, $1,500 down. They'd blanched, begged for a night's consideration, and were silent all the way back to the Dome.

But now they were back. I stood up smiling and put out my hand, and Mr. Willard, nodding nervously, shepherded his wife past my desk to Doreen's.

I sat down again. Doreen was a very pretty girl a little younger than myself, a capable receptionist but—even if she *was* showing me the ropes—not a salesman. There were no female salesmen, of course.

The one thing Doreen had neglected to teach me was how to poach someone else's client. She took the Willards behind the scenes for an hour before walking them to the door and giving them a showy send-off.

So I sat studying floor plans, answered the phone the few times it rang, watched out for walk-ins, bade the Ravens goodnight as their chauffeurs pulled up their respective Cadillacs nose-to-tail for the trip to Holmby Hills, and at 5:00 o'clock went home myself.

The Depression was awful, of course, a disaster, a nightmare you couldn't wake up from or kick free of, but in our office, at least, it had its leisurely aspect, too.

As usual Doreen and I walked together down to our Red Car stop on Santa Monica Boulevard. She lived in Hollywood, and I further east in Pasadena, so we could share the first leg of my epic trip home.

"I saw the Willards," I told her once we were seated.

"Yes, Bing, sorry about that," she said. "And thanks for taking care of them yesterday: You set the hook. Not landed yet, but they're thinking about it. She was a suffragette, that's why they wanted me.

"But Bing, some people, when they come in with questions, they're looking for information, sure, but also want a guide, a helping hand, *encouragement*. Reassurance they're doing the right thing spending so much on themselves. Goodness me, $3,000 just for a lot! Ten or twelve thousand more for a house! Some of our customers might find you a little intense, a little too serious."

"The curse of being an engineer."

I smiled, but she was right. Selling real estate wasn't my calling, and never would be. My calling was engineering, but where were there any jobs in it?

We were coming up to her stop, Western Avenue.

"But you'll get the hang of it, I know you will," she said. "'Night, Bing."

"'Night, Doreen."

Several blocks up, almost catty-corner from the Central Casting building at Hollywood Boulevard, I could see the boarding house where her mother rented rooms to aspiring actresses come to try their luck in Tinsel Town.

It occurred to me I should ask Doreen out.

2.

THOUGH MY JOB at the Dome wasn't a good fit, having any job at all was a godsend. Mine came about through my uncle, Jim Groves.

I wrote about Uncle Jim in *The Last Posse,* if you read it. In 1922 he was Sheriff of Texas' Wilbarger County when, 12-year-old me at his side, he led the posse that by automobile and on horseback tracked down and captured Frank Holloway, the notorious *Oklahoma Yeggman* with seven notches on his guns, one for every man he'd killed. Uncle Jim helped me grow up at that challenging age; little did I know he was about to wake me up at the grown but slumbrous age of 25.

I'd come home to Dad's in the middle of August a fresh Ohio State University Ph.D. in chemical engineering. Matriculating in 1928 at 18, I'd earned my bachelor's degree, my master's, finally my doctorate with a dissertation on *Behavior of Waxes in High-Temperature Environments.* Won't bore you with the details, but it's in the petrochemical line of things.

I loved the field, loved school, loved plowing my way through the requirements, helped at first by Dad, then – when the Depression started to bite – taking campus jobs, summer jobs and finding scholarships and assistantships. Now I opened my eyes for the first time in seven years, a new-minted doctor ready to snatch up a job with brilliant prospects – and there weren't any.

No jobs. None, not anywhere, even for a *cum laude* Ph.D. from OSU! Not in Texas, nor Pennsylvania, not in Ohio or Louisiana. The country so prosperous when I plunged into my studies was, when I emerged, a poorer, more sullen place where, if I wanted to eat, I had to put my training aside and take whatever I could get.

Luckily, Dad welcomed me home. He was a schoolteacher, respected and senior, and my step-mother Violet was a popular teacher as well, and though I remember from my earliest days Mom and Dad (she taught, too, until her death) saying they'd never get rich, the job was steady and, in Pasadena even in the Depression, secure. Pasadena's better off than you might know and, to the eye, at least, the Depression didn't change that. While the rest of Los Angeles seemed to lose vibrancy and color, to go from Technicolor to black-and-white, Pasadena retained what it had before, something of the silents' glamorous silver.

At Sunday supper the week of my tail-between-my-legs homecoming, Uncle Jim congratulated me on completing my studies and took to calling me *Doc*. Which I could have done without. But kindly as ever, and apparently glad to see his little deputy again.

He was my Mom's favorite brother, and always great friends with Dad. Despite being in California for three years, but for the missing star he was still every inch the formidable figure he'd been when we tore off across the Panhandle in pursuit of Frank Holloway. Of course he was older now, in his 50s, thicker, thin on top, mustache gray, peering out from creased, sunburned skin.

In other words, a hayseed in a white Stetson, twill shirt, bolo tie, fringed jacket and dungarees. Embarrassing, considering we weren't in Texas any longer, but in California. At least he'd given up cowboy boots for a crepe-soled shoe easier on his feet. To me, his get-up made him look like a hick.

We reminisced about his putting me into long pants after I arrived in Vernon wearing short pants; part of his overhaul that took me from spoiled pretty boy to toughened-up kid who knew better how to take things as they come.

And after hearing my tale of woe, Uncle Jim said he'd talk to his boss about finding me a job. This startled me, but I was willing. What kind of job, though?

He was working, he said, for a Holmby Hills family that had a real-estate business. Said they were always on the lookout for bright youngsters. And what did *he* do for them? He was their night watchman. *Watchman?* Seemed a comedown to me, though I didn't say anything.

"But why would they give *me* a job?"

"Don't sell yourself short, Doc," said Jim. "I'll speak with Mr. Thomas Raven and let you know."

Good as his word, he called a few days later and told me when to present myself at the Dome in Westwood Village. I duly met Mr. Raven and his brother, was hired and started the following Monday.

It was a job, and I was happy to hand over my weekly draw to Dad as rent, and grateful to Uncle Jim, but after three weeks I had yet to earn my first commission and knew that selling real estate wasn't for me.

THE SUNDAY FOLLOWING my personal encounter with Andrew Cassidy, Jim came over to Dad's as usual. After eating Violet's famous roast beef we resumed the Monopoly game that had already consumed two Sundays. It was new that year, in the depths of the Depression. No one had any money, so getting notionally rich in railroads or hotels was very appealing.

I'd been waiting for this moment to regale everybody with

the Monopoly man's visit to the Dome, and soon had them in stitches—but unexpectedly it stirred stuff up, too.

Jim growled, "Malevolent old bastard." Immediately he apologized. "Sorry, Violet, that just slipped out."

"No more than the truth, Jim," she asserted in a way strong for her, and to my amazement there emerged the story of how Cassidy harmed her people years earlier when he was buying drilling rights on Signal Hill in Long Beach, and getting them for a song since no one suspected there might be oil in the ground there.

But Cassidy's uncanny instincts told him that petroleum lay beneath Violet's parents' bungalow. They took his modest offering of cash, and before they knew it derricks sprouted from front lawn and back yard and they had to move out. A few royalty cheques that soon ceased didn't make up for the loss of their home.

"Lots of stories like that about Cassidy," Dad murmured.

"Thought he was supposed to be some great philanthropist," I said. "Cassidy Library? Easy touch for Catholic charities?"

They filled me in on how Cassidy amassed his money in the first place—on his decades of taking and grabbing, bald-faced thievery, bribery, *murder*, and how throughout his career he'd impoverished anyone fool enough to become his partner.

His masterpiece was going to be the Teapot Dome. To get his hands on the U.S. Navy's oil reserves, he bribed the Secretary of the Interior. Who went to prison. While Cassidy got off scot-free.

"Scot-free, 'less you count his son," Jim noted. "For no good reason made his son his bagman—had him deliver $100,000 *cash* to the Secretary. Then on the eve of telling Congress all about it, the son ends up on the oriental rug of his bedroom in Beverly Hills with a bullet in his brain. With his secretary-*friend* lying a dozen feet off in a similar condition."

Why didn't I know about this? Oh yes, my years studying at

Ohio State.

"Suicide? Murder?"

"Both, I'd say," Jim replied. "Apple doesn't fall far. Cassidy's one of those where everybody in the vicinity's going to come to a bad end. If he's alive, he's stealing and killing. He'll stop only when he's dead."

From my mellow uncle this was so surprising a speech that I stared.

"Memory serves, Jim," Dad said gently, "you had dealings with Cassidy yourself?"

"Years ago," he answered, "and I do not care for the man."

And speaking slowly, in a rumbling voice that compelled attention, Uncle Jim explained how, after deciding he was getting too old to be Sheriff, he went into the oil business with his brother Eustace. In those days there was quite a bit of oil around Vernon, Texas. The famous Electra oilfield on the Waggoner Ranch south of town was near the ranch where Jim and Eustace grew up.

The brothers leased land west of town, drilled—and hit oil. Not a big producer, only about 100 barrels a day, but it made them think they'd found a new field. Looking around for capital to drill another well, they met a man in Wichita Falls who advanced what they needed. He didn't volunteer whose agent he was, so they didn't know that accidentally they'd taken Andrew Cassidy into partnership.

In defiance of wildcatter's luck, their second well was a gusher. It was giving them 2,000 barrels a day, a taste of wealth, and Uncle Jim had just bought a ten-room brick house on Pease Street in Vernon, when Cassidy's Pan-Hemispheric Petroleum rolled in and started drilling on adjacent leases—and soon Jim's and Eustace's gusher was dribbling out only ten barrels a day, then five, before going dry altogether, while new pumpjacks surrounding their wells sawed away merrily.

Jim and Eustace found themselves on the outside looking in on their own venture. Royalties docked to pay back their silent partner, their debts soaring beyond any possibility of repayment, they underwent the exquisite humiliation of declaring bankruptcy. Jim lost the house and part of his home ranch in nearby Bugscuffle. Luck of the game, Cassidy's people told him.

Can't say I followed every detail of Uncle Jim's story. The oil business is very complicated. But the upshot was that thanks to Cassidy he lost his shirt; but for Andrew Cassidy, he'd be a rich man today.

"Why he bothered with my two-bit affair, I'll never know. Think a man with two hundred million could let the little guy alone once in a while."

"Did you say two hundred *million?*" I asked. *"Dollars?"*

"Hell, yes, Doc: *dollars.*"

"Well," I said after a suitable silence, "he'll be even richer if USC beats UCLA next month: Made a $10 bet with the Ravens."

"Did he now? Ten bucks?"

"Yep, ten shares in the Caldego Oil Company, $1 par value per share."

Uncle Jim sat back, looking surprised.

"Caldego," he said. "Don't mean to brag, but that's down to me, too. Caldego Canyon's up from Castaic, past the Valley? The Ravens own a big tract and, what with the Depression, can't develop it yet, but I was up there with them one day and happened to remark—should learn to keep my big mouth shut—that it looked like oil country to me.

"Well, they actually brought in people who agreed, drilled a well, hit oil—and it was pretty much my experience all over again. In the oil game—trust me—a lot of money goes out before anything comes in. Another time, they might have built it up slow, learned the business as they went, but they decided to approach the biggest oilman around, and he was only too happy to oblige. So Caldego Oil's their joint venture with Cassidy — own it 50-50. But probably Cassidy's getting most of the benefit.

"Told the Ravens that despite his butter-wouldn't-melt, sweet-old-man appearance, Cassidy's a crook, a viper, a *killer*. Yes, they said, but he knows oil and we don't, so stay out of it. So I do."

After Jim went home, Dad remarked that he'd never heard the full story of his oil venture.

"Made him a bitter man, and I'm sorry to see it."

3.

THE FOLLOWING THURSDAY, I picked up the phone at the Dome to hear Uncle Jim inviting me out to *his* place for Saturday lunch.

Curious to see what kind of set-up he had, living in a cottage behind Mr. Thomas's home, I borrowed Dad's Chevy and drove west through glorious September sunshine, feeling lucky indeed. *Who'd a-thunk it a month ago, Bing? You have landed on your feet!*

In those days the Los Angeles Basin was still mostly ranchland and farmland, dotted by small towns like Hollywood and Culver City — not all that different from Ohio's countryside, if browner. On the two-lane Santa Monica Boulevard — Red Car tracks alongside it — Beverly Hills was the first town after Hollywood, separated from it by bean fields and orange groves. Then you hit a scattering of stores, big new houses rising over big lawns, bigger ones behind walls and hedges and a hilly district of mansions, hardly visible.

In the part of it called Holmby Hills I followed Sunset Boulevard to North Carolwood Drive, and turned in through the wrought-iron gates Uncle Jim told me about, guarded by a lodge where one of his men gave me a gander and a wave. Up the drive I went.

It was lovely, everything manicured like a park, lawns

emerald in the sun and not a sound except for the birds. At the uphill curve Mr. Thomas's house came into view — *huge,* a Tudor of stone and brick with slate roofs, diamond-paned windows, terraces bounded by stone urns. I stopped and sat a minute to admire it, until crows cawing overhead gave me a chill of foreboding — that menacing disquiet that in Southern California can jump you unawares, give you goosebumps.

After the turning Uncle Jim mentioned I found a line of houses built in similar but scaled-down style. Pulling up beside the last one — bigger than Dad's — I saw men opposite washing and polishing a collection of Cadillacs and Duesenbergs. Splashing of a different sort came across a hedge in the back yard, with howls of laughter.

As I went up the walkway, the front door opened and Jim called, "Morning, Doc. Find us OK?"

"No trouble a-tall. Say Uncle Jim, is this where you live? Gee, you've landed in a tub of *butter.* Thought you said you had a *cottage.*"

I was in a stone-floored, two-storied foyer, the walls a fancy plaster with iron sconces. Taking me into a living room with a stone hearth and leather couches, Jim sat down in an armchair.

"Well, it *is* a cottage — the five-bedroom kind. But you saw Mr. Thomas's house coming up the drive? We're going over in a minute — boss man wants to see you — so you'll see for yourself. Mr. Delbert's is just as grand, and so's their sister's over on Charing Cross Road. Makes for a kind of family compound, you see."

"What is it you do here, Uncle Jim?"

"Well, Mr. Thomas has a daughter, so like all these folks since the Lindbergh baby he worries about kidnapers. General security 'bout sums it up."

Eyes unfocussed, he looked out the window, and I gathered there were ins-and-outs to "general security" it wasn't necessary to tell me about.

Screams of pleasure came over the hedge.

"Everything's got a cost, Doc," Jim blurted out. "Everything in life's got a price tag. Just make sure there's never a price tag on *you*."

This was peculiar, but I just asked, "That a swimming pool I hear?"

"Oh, didn't I tell you? Shorty lives here with me. Or is it vice-versa?"

"*Shorty?*" Shorty was his youngest son, my slightly older cousin. "How *is* ol' Shorty?"

"Doing real good. Just back from football camp. Starting fullback on the Bruins again this year."

I had to blink at that. Playing college ball at 25?

"Only thing is, Doc — and it's real important — everyone calls him 'Ted' now. He's 'Texas Ted.'"

"*'Texas Ted'?* Then what're you calling *Ted?*" I asked, smartass that I am. Ted was his middle son, still back in Vernon, far as I knew.

"Tell you 'bout it later, only remember to call him Ted."

"Okey-doke, Uncle Jim," I said, though I don't promise I didn't also roll my eyes.

"Well, let's go see Mr. Thomas."

Getting up, he put on his Stetson and I my fedora. In Los Angeles you need something on your head between April and October; the glare's just too terrific. In Ohio, where the light's northern, flatter, mediated by humidity and four distinct seasons, I'd forgotten the sheer weight of the light in California.

Going out the back door and crossing the veranda and lawn, we found a passage through the hedge and emerged onto a terrace surrounding a big blue swimming pool. Behind it stood the rear of the Tudor mansion I'd admired from the drive.

And there was Shorty, propped up on an elbow like an

ancient river god in a blue-and-gold bathing suit, its straps lying carelessly across his shoulders. That first shot of John Wayne in *Stagecoach*? Something like that. A big, lazy-looking galoot, my cousin, and *beautiful*. A pretty dark-haired girl kneeled adoringly in front of him. At first I took her to be his age, but every glance took off a year.

"Ted, someone you'll want to see," called Jim.

Shorty took me in, eyes quick as his dad's, but letting his features play catch-up, looking glad to see me in an idle, don't-mean-ever-to-move kind of way.

"Hey Bing, little boy last time I saw *you*," he drawled. "Grown up good!"

We shook hands. His were like hams.

"Could say the same about you, Sho — *Ted*. How you doing?"

"Oh, can't complain."

"'Sho-*Ted*,'" said the girl, face glinting with amusement. "You from the South, *honeychile?*"

"Doc, this is Miss Ruth Raven," said Jim.

"Miss Raven."

"Glad to meet you, '*Doc.*' My, Jim, you have such a good-looking family."

"Thank you, Miss Raven. Come on, Doc, this way."

4.

GOLLY, WAS THAT HOUSE BIG! Everything twice life-size, rooms receding into the distance. It intimidated me, but Jim seemed at home as he led me along first one corridor, then another, finally knocking at an arched oaken door studded with ironwork.

"Come in!"

We found Mr. Thomas seated at a desk in a beamed room, oversized furniture all around. Remaining seated, he pointed out a chair for me, while Jim sat down by the fireplace.

"Bing, thanks for dropping by on your day off," he said. "Something we wanted to talk to you about, my brother and I. Mr. Cassidy's coming by the Dome the other day put us on to it.

"Now, we know you're doing your best with us: very conscientious, very thorough. Well, but you're a chemist by training, correct?"

"Yes, sir, my degrees are in chemical engineering, with a specialty in waxes—"

"Fascinating. But you'd know your way around an oilfield and refinery?"

"Oh, yes, sir."

"Well, as it happens— You've heard of this Caldego Oil Company? See, we own land up past the Valley where eventually we mean to build homes. Anyway, upshot is we brought Cassidy in—Mr. Cassidy—to help us develop it in the meantime as an oilfield, and now we've got some 15 wells pumping away. Share the profits even-steven. Pretty good profits, too."

"Yes, sir."

He was tense—the way people are when things aren't quite right.

"Long and short of it, Bing, my brother and I would like you to transfer to Caldego Oil. They're Downtown in the old Cassidy Oil building on Broadway. Offices are up in the new Pan-Hemispheric building on Bunker Hill—the one with the searchlight on the roof?—but the real work goes on in the labs down on Broadway. Caldego Canyon's crude gets carried by rail down to the refinery in Long Beach, but Downtown keeps tabs on everything.

"Your job would be to test the product, file reports with the State, help keep wells and refinery running smoothly, and so forth. Whatever they require.

"Want you to be our man on the inside, you might say—keep an eye on our interests for us, let us know what's going on. Cassidy brings us a cheque every month, carries it to the Dome in a big show—you saw—but every month he brings us a little less than the month before.

"We go out to the field and count what there is to count—more derricks, pumpjacks, trucks, tanks, roughnecks every time, but the cheques keep shrinking. Claims it's expenses for more piping, more tanks, more *mud*. You have no idea how expensive *mud* can be. Says the oil's running out, anyhow. We seconded an accountant of ours—Mr. Browning—up there a few months back, but he can't seem to figure things out. Keeps going on about truck odometers.

"That's where *you* come in. Now, Cassidy knows oil. We don't. Had to take him on as partner, but he's a crook. Oh, the

Archbishop might disagree, even USC's trustees, but we're talking about a man who's left a trail of bodies behind him since 1890."

Did I like the sound of that? Not particularly.

"Had to get in bed with the devil to do this deal. To Cassidy, Caldego's small potatoes. So he waltzes in every month waving a cheque at us, how do we know it represents our half of the profits? We *don't*. We're dependent on the good faith of a *crook*.

"So we need to know just how much business Caldego's doing, Bing: The real numbers. Would you help us with that?"

"Sure. Yes, sir. Do my best."

"Good man."

And he looked relieved. His shoulders came down, so did his voice and he nodded at Uncle Jim.

"Now look, my brother called up Cassidy, asked about a job for you. Might smell a rat, I don't know. Might think you're our ringer. Which you are, but you've got your degrees and letters of recommendation. Here's one from us, glowing as can be after so short a time."

He handed me an envelope.

"And don't worry, we'll keep your draw going, as if you were still at the Dome. How much is it?"

"Twenty-fi—"

"We'll keep that up, so whatever Caldego pays will be gravy. Sound all right?"

"Yes, sir." In fact, it sounded *too* good. A little fishy.

"Plus— You have a car?"

"No, sir."

"Need a car." Pulling out a drawer, he came up with a fistful of greenbacks. "Here's $300. Go get yourself an old Dodge or Ford."

"Yes, sir. Thank you, sir."

"Well, good then. Don't know how long we'll want to keep

you there. Up your alley, anyway."

"Yes, sir, I'll get a car, and come by the Dome to clear out my desk and say goodbye to everyone."

He gave me a puzzled look, then muttered, "Oh, *Doreen.*"

Gathering my courage, I said, "Mr. Raven, you should promote Doreen — make her a salesman. She'd be good."

He looked surprised, even taken aback, but said, "Might be an idea at that. Jim, thanks for bringing your nephew by."

Jim got to his feet and I shook hands with Mr. Raven, who nodded us out a French door to the terrace as cries erupted from the pool. Passing from cool shadow to sunlight that instantly struck off color and detail — leaving only shape until our eyes adjusted — we skirted the pool, where the river god, stoically afloat on a rubber raft, was being splashed by the girl hanging onto it. Then he launched himself at her, coming up under her and lifting her high on his shoulders to her screams of delight.

"Sandwich sound good?" asked Jim.

Finding our way through the hedge, we returned to Jim's cottage. It certainly was a fine house, Jim's was, with all the accoutrements you want in a Tudor.

We settled in the kitchen. Jim produced two bottles of Balboa beer and made me the best ham sandwich I ever ate.

"You like Mr. Thomas's idea, Doc?"

"Yes, I do, Uncle Jim. I'm no salesman. Doreen's trying to help me do better, but what I really am is a petroleum engineer."

"Seen her at the Dome. Pretty gal."

"Jim, how'd the Ravens get all this, anyway?"

More screams rang out from the pool. After they died down, he said, "Well, the brothers are second generation in the land game. Dad came from England, was a doctor till he noticed how many people were streaming into Los Angeles."

He pronounced it as though referring to a trigonometry problem: *Angleiss;* the common pronunciation in those days.

"Started buying land and building houses in Boyle Heights, but even 30 years ago could see money moving west off Bunker Hill. Began building in Hollywood and Hancock Park. Did real well."

"They're millionaires?"

"*Multimillionaires*. Thing about real estate, though, is it has its cycles – goes up, goes down. Never been so low as now. House worth $5,000 in '29? Lucky to get *two* today, if anyone will buy at all. So the brothers are feeling the pinch. Work on a bigger scale than their dad ever did, but just at the moment they're land rich and cash poor."

"How bad a pinch?"

"Well, trying to sell off what they can, pennies on the dollar, and letting go some staff." A tip of his head included Mr. Delbert's and their sister's. "Had me lay off a man, and they're that concerned with security it shows they're hurting.

"Mind, their assets are tremendous: They own Westwood Village and Holmby Hills outright, big slices of Hancock Park, Beverly Hills, Brentwood, Bel Air, the Valley, Santa Monica, Malibu, what have you. Not to mention apartment houses on Wilshire, houses in Hollywood, Silver Lake, Boyle Heights, plus Caldego Canyon and who knows what else.

"Few years ago their real estate was throwing up gushers of cash, but that's dried up now. Property taxes must be bleeding them dry. Never saw the Depression coming – no one in California did. And it's not so bad here as other places. My land, Doc, our people in Texas? Hurtin' *bad*.

"The Ravens might be in rough shape, but the last thing they'll do is let anyone see it. Front's as big in real estate as sports."

"So why'd they hire *me*?"

"Well, I asked them to."

"Jim, why's Shorty going by *Ted*?"

"Now that's a long story."
He chewed his sandwich.
"Best ham there is," he said. *"Smithfield."*

5.

UNLIKE SOME WHO TELL YOU something's a long story just to change the subject, Jim finished his sandwich, wiped his mouth with the napkin tucked, hick-style, into his shirt, leaned back and told me all about it.

"Big UCLA boosters, the Raven brothers — the biggest. Hell, it only exists where it does 'cause the Ravens got it there. Stories about how they managed, which I won't go into. But that big, beautiful campus? Sold it to the State for a song.

"Mr. Thomas is convinced UCLA's going to be the making of Westwood Village. Always sees the sunny side of things."

"And Mr. Delbert?"

He sighed. "Well, Mr. Delbert tends to see the shady side. Maybe that's what makes them a good team."

He broke off as squeals of laughter came closer and Miss Raven pattered screeching through the kitchen, leaving wet footprints on the tile, Shorty barreling after and making a feint for her across the table, catching her at the swinging door to the dining room, flipping her over his shoulder and carrying her off shrieking.

The door swung shut.

"OK: *Ted.* Well, country's crazy 'bout college ball, and across town USC's made itself into a powerhouse — oh, purely through Cassidy's money. Team was garbage till his son started pumping cash into it. The old man keeps it up in his memory, buying them the biggest farm boys and miners anyone can find. Turned the program around.

"Ravens want to *beat* him—so they've gone and bought themselves a team, too."

"*Ah*," I said.

"Shorty—*Ted*—is their fullback. Best you ever saw. Have some other good players—wait till you see Chuck Cheshire!— and with any luck should be Pacific Coast Conference champs this year, Rose Bowl and everything. But to do it's costing the Ravens a good deal of what's in short supply just now.

"Make the Bruins champs, the glory will rub off on Westwood Village and their houses will sell like hot cakes. That's the plan, and they know their game. Plus they do just love UCLA. But, Doc, Ted's the key to the whole shebang."

"So how long has *Ted* been playing ball?"

"Let's see. Played at Vernon High, of course, then for Terrill Prep in Dallas with his brothers. Weatherford Junior College. Texas School of Mines starting in. . . in '30, was it? Out here in '32, when the Ravens discovered him.

"Put him in at their feeder school, Urban Military Academy in Santa Monica, as a senior named 'Rodney Vernon Maness'— friend back home. That's when I came out. Gave me a job and this house to live in. *Cottage*. Real lucky for us.

"The Ravens have played it smart, recruiting carefully, hiring good coaches. With Ted in there, feel pretty sure of their season.

"First year he was on the practice squad because of a little mix-up at Urban Military: Got called on the matter of 'Rodney Vernon Maness.' Confessed to using a fake name 'cause his folks didn't want him playing ball, that really he was Ted Groves. Good as any other name, I guess.

"Look, eligibility's complicated—and unfair: Lose a year just transferring? Problem started when he graduated from Vernon without enough credits for college, and no one's ever helped him get any: All anyone's wanted to do is put him on the field.

"Anyway, UCLA's had some bad seasons. Nothing surprising about that, it's new and full of wispy California boys. Started an annual game with USC five years back, but the Trojans smashed 'em up so bad in the first two, series was cancelled. So next month's game is the first since then."

The telephone rang, one ring. Presumably Ted answered it.

"Ted—his brother Ted—OK with all this?"

"Oh sure. Chicken farming back in Vernon, happy as a clam. Proud of his brother."

"Isn't it kind of risky, Uncle Jim?"

He was slow to answer. "Ted gets unmasked, that's the end of *this*, I imagine." His head inclined. "But it beats starving back in Bugscuffle. Know what they're calling Bugscuffle these days? Now officially *Elliott*, Texas."

"Is it really?"

He got up and I followed him into the living room. Ted and Miss Raven were lounging on towels on the couch, she halfway onto his lap, giggling.

Before we could sit down Ted said, "Dad, Mr. Delbert just called over. He'd like a word with Bing, too."

Jim got his hat. "I'll show you the way, Doc."

"Like football, Bing?" Ted called. "You want, can get you into the games."

"Great! Thanks, Sho—*Ted*."

6.

TAKING ME OUT BACK again, Jim found a flagstone path that took us through glades and gardens.

Squeals erupted behind us.

"Ted sweet on her?" I asked.

"Better not be, Doc. Sixteen years old."

"Her father have eyes in his head?"

"Some question as to that."

A minute later we were coming up behind another vast Tudor mansion. I was getting used to them by now. On its terrace Mr. Delbert sat at a table whose blue-and-gold umbrella put his face in shadow. Next to him was a lady I recognized.

"Damn," Jim said. "Got his fancy woman with him."

"That's Mrs. Andrew Cassidy!" I exclaimed. And a few seconds later, "They're having an *affair?* Isn't that *dangerous?*"

"Imagine that's the fun of it. Well, there you go."

He ducked back into the greenery and I crossed the lawn. It was beautiful, that grass, those gardens, birds calling, the house looming over everything. Then a crow cawed, and that flicker of dread announced itself. In the whole scene the only thing moving was Mr. Delbert pouring coffee for his lady friend. He rang a handbell and a Mexican man in a white jacket brought a fresh carafe and took the old one away.

"Ah, Bing," he called. "Come on up, take a seat."

I sat down and scooched my chair into the shade, which felt good. My hat I rested on an empty chair. Mrs. Cassidy, fair and shining in her nest of furs, went unintroduced, so I ignored her as best I could. Up close she was, if beautiful, fidgety with blinks and grimaces.

Mr. Delbert got right to it.

"Grateful you're doing this for us, Bing. Do what Cassidy tells you and you'll learn a lot. He was impressed — *mighty* impressed — by your degrees, but remember, what he knows didn't come from a book, and what he knows, he *knows*. You'll be getting a post-doc course in real life."

He barked a laugh before continuing.

"My brother fill you in? We want to know what the hell's going on. Don't intend to be cheated. Now, you won't get anywhere near Cassidy's books — runs his accounting out of Pan-Hemispheric on Bunker Hill."

"And wouldn't know what I was looking at if I saw them," I interjected.

He nodded. "But find out what you can, we'll have a better idea about things."

He and his brother were at an age — 40 or so — where their looks were beginning to diverge. Mr. Thomas had already put on a few jolly pounds to go with his optimistic eyes. Mr. Delbert seemed likelier to go the other way, his cheeks hollowed out with feeding the fires of resentment in his eyes. By contrast, Mrs. Cassidy was cool — cool as ice, as suggested by her platinum hair and frozen pendants at ears and throat.

He drained his cup and rang. The Mexican man carried cups and carafe away and brought out two glasses and a pitcher of orange juice. No one offered me anything.

"What's that boy of ours up to over there? Could hear him from here."

"Went for a swim."

"Now, this bet with Cassidy that you witnessed," he said. "Repercussions if we lose."

"Really?" I asked. "Ten bucks on a football game?"

Mrs. Cassidy laughed out loud and Mr. Delbert smiled sardonically.

"Ten bucks, yeah, that's right. Anyway, not your department. Cassidy's bought himself a team of professional gorillas—*again*. Nothing we can do, except do the same. Your cousin's Exhibit A. Exhibit A-*plus*. Finally convinced my brother that's how the game is played. Can't put 20-year-olds up against Cassidy's thugs.

"So we've got an excellent chance. Seen your cousin play ball? Helluva player.

"Important that you pass on what you hear about the Trojans, too. May not hear anything—but on the other hand. Don't worry, we've got eyes on their practices, even someone the coach likes— Well, don't need to know that.

"Going to be a busy fall for you, Bing, that's what I'm saying. OK, first off, go see Cassidy."

"*Me*, see Mr. Cassidy?"

"Meets every new employee. He's expecting you, over there in West Adams. Stays on in that old house like it's the height of fashion." He snorted. "And maybe it *was*—in 1900."

He gave me the address.

"All right, can go now. Good luck."

I went. Mrs. Cassidy looked glad of it.

7.

BACK AT THE COTTAGE I thanked Uncle Jim for lunch and told him I was off to meet Cassidy himself.

"God, what won't millionaires do when they start feeling *poor?*" he said, walking me out to the Chevy. "Look, want to give this deal some thought?"

"Nah," I said. "Double salary and a *car?*"

Sure, there were things to watch out for, pay attention to, but they didn't worry me—I was 25 and that eager to get into the petrochemical industry. And Jim was forgetting I'd already had the pleasure of sizing up the Oil King. *Killer?* The husk of one. Didn't scare me.

"Well, suggest you keep it under your hat that Mrs. Cassidy's over here. Playing with fire with that one."

"Or ice."

Starting the car, I found the nerve to say what I'd been meaning to.

"Uncle Jim, this imposture of Shorty's—"

"This *what?*"

"Pretending to be *Ted*. Doesn't that bother you?"

"Doc, you're young, and in case you haven't noticed, there's a Depression on. Think he'd have money for college without football?"

All right, not up for discussion, yet I was sorry to see my old hero involved in anything that, however necessitous, was less than honest. But so far as it's being the Depression, he was on the money. What could I do?

Driving downhill and dropping over to Exposition Boulevard, I headed east. Not a neighborhood I'd visited for years. Admired the enormous Coliseum — Rome's isn't a patch on ours — and crossed USC's handsome campus, more verdant than UCLA's. Cassidy Library's campanile soared over everything.

Winding up South Figueroa to West Adams, past the magnificent St. Vincent de Paul's Church — a Cassidy benefaction grander than most cathedrals — I reached Cassidy's gates. There a man asked my name, poked his head over my lap to read the steering wheel's registration card and spoke into a telephone, before nodding me on through a grove of eucalyptus trees. I know some think their turpentine tang healthful.

And there arose an old brick house trimmed with stone, gabled wings embracing a flagged area around a fountain. Another officious little man pointed where to park and without a word escorted me to the porte-cochère, where yet another held out his hand for my hat.

"Follow me," said this one. "He's in with his martyrs."

We progressed down what resembled a nave. Color from stained-glass windows splashed needlepoint chairs and the teak floorboards. My guide knocked on a linenfold door, preceded me inside and took his place at the wall.

I stood in what at first I took for a chapel, but in fact was Cassidy's library, few books on view but with many big paintings — religious pictures that made it a torture chamber. Here St. Lawrence sizzled on a gridiron, there St. Agnes's head was lopped off, St. Bartholomew flayed alive, St. Peter crucified, St. Stephen stoned. Amidst silent screams, heads and limbs flew in gouts of blood. Broken on her wheel, St. Catherine managed a remarkable composure, but I felt uncomfortable, to say the least.

"Welcome to my private heaven," rasped the Monopoly man. "Take it you're *Bing?*"

Shrewdness suffusing his features, Cassidy was seated in a red-velvet armchair like a Renaissance Pope, his monocled eye — a hole to licking flames — fixed on me.

"Yes, sir," I said, but had to break off my gaze. Which was a mistake, for he scoffed, opening his mouth to a sharpened yellow palisade.

"So you want to work for Caldego Oil?"

"Yes, sir."

"Heard about your degrees. Got a letter of recommendation?" I handed it over and he took a look, sniffing, "Any *practical* experience?"

"Oh, yes, sir," I assured him. "Spent the summers of '31 and '32 at Colorado Fuel and Iron in Pueblo, Colorado."

"Two whole summers, eh? Never finished school, myself. Tell me, drill through 1,000, 2,000 feet of the Pleistocene, what do you find beneath?"

"The upper Miocene — what around here they call the Fernando formation."

"Say you've placed a wooden plug in a well at 1,700 feet and filled it with 200 feet of soil, but you still have water. What do you do?"

"I'd try pumping cement into the hole and back into the surrounding structures, though you could also — "

"What's casing-head gasoline?"

"It's an incidental product — incidental to compressing natural gas before it's transported."

"What do you do with it?"

"Well, put it in the pipeline, recover it at the refinery."

"No pipeline out of Caldego Canyon, wouldn't pay to lay

143

one, so just put casing-head gas into the collection tanks," he instructed. "So you're such a lousy salesman the Ravens want to get rid of you, eh?"

"I'm *not —*"

"Saw you at that tomb of theirs, *'The Dome.'* Must be hurting? Business slow?"

"Wouldn't know about that, sir."

"Sorry my wife's not back from Mass yet, you should meet her. Oh, wouldn't she make *you* hot and bothered?" He licked his lips. "People laughed when I married Margery. Oh, I know, they *laughed.* But Margery's Roman Catholic and *devout.* Beauty of being Catholic is you can do anything you want with no consequences so long as you're *sorry.* Probably shouldn't let *that* cat out of the bag, but I assure you, and my confessor, good Father Dugan, that I'm *sincerely* sorry."

He chortled.

"Margery's for my afterlife, you see. Comes of long-lived stock, should have 50, 60 years praying for my soul, having Masses and rosaries said for it, overseeing my bequests to dear Mother Church. So even if dear God should place me in Purgatory before welcoming me through the pearly gates, my stay there will be brief. Always was a chalice-half-full sort of fellow."

Eyes glittering, he smirked: Had it all figured out.

"Eight-thirty, Monday morning. Know where we are? Cassidy Oil building, Broadway near Pico. Corporate headquarters is on Bunker Hill — that's *not* where you'll be.

"What you'll find — with all your admirable *schooling* — is that we do things a certain way that's taken form, evolved over my entire career, because it *works.*"

"Yes, sir."

"Just do things our way — *my* way — and you'll get along fine. Thirty dollars a week."

"Yes, sir. Thank you, sir."
He nodded in dismissal.

8.

MONDAY MORNING I DROVE downtown in my brand-new (to me) 1930 Model A Ford, a nice number in green I picked up on Colorado Boulevard Saturday evening for $295 and gassed up at a Pan-Hemispheric station, feeling proprietary watching the famous orange-dyed gasoline pour through the tubes. Still felt proprietary going down Broadway; against all odds, I had a job in my own profession!

Office buildings ten stories tall lined Broadway, along with department stores, movie palaces and restaurants. Streetcars passed every minute, and crowds swarmed the sidewalks, while auto traffic was glacial. Glimpsing City Hall and St. Vibiana's Cathedral, I passed the Los Angeles *Times'* new limestone monolith. Waiting through a light beside the Metropolitan building let me admire, up Bunker Hill, Pan-Hemispheric Petroleum's headquarters; its revolving rooftop light was quenched, however, it being daytime. I waited through a light beside the Examiner building, Hearst's terra-cotta showcase.

Rich as Hearst was, he wasn't as rich as my new boss. But you wouldn't know it from the battered brick building at Pico whose inset panel proclaimed CASSIDY OIL CO. Parking behind it and going inside, I was directed upstairs. All three floors contained laboratories, each dedicated to a different oilfield.

I found Caldego Canyon's room on the top floor, skylights overhead, counters and benches on the linoleum arranged in work stations with Bunsen burners, beakers, reactors, microscopes, bookcases filled with bottles and reports. I breathed deep: Home at last.

"New guy," said a pleasant-looking fellow with a rock-hard handshake. He was my immediate boss, what was called a floor manager. "Bing? Vince. Come on in. Sorry it's so jammed — taking over part of Sansisena next door soon, that'll give you more space."

"Thought Caldego Canyon was a dying field?"

"Where'd you hear *that?* No, good producer, expanding pretty fast. Here's the set-up: We get samples in on a daily basis — this being Monday, means Friday's are waiting for you. Saturday's and Sunday's come in around lunchtime.

"What we need to know first off is sulfur content, 'cause there's an issue — Caldego Canyon's borderline sulfurous. We can cope, but before the refinery — that's down in Long Beach, runs like a top, very proud of that plant — before Long Beach starts cracking it they need to know what they're up against. Follow?"

I followed, followed happily, for this was where I belonged. My analyses would be forwarded to the refinery and the Bunker Hill offices, and summed up every month in a report filed with the State. The quarterly *California Mineral Production Bulletin* published summaries of every well's output and its constituent elements, so everything had to be on the up-and-up.

Vince said the State's main interest was taxation.

Also I met my lab technician, a pimply young Mexican named Luis, a high-school graduate with a good head on his shoulders and a deft way with lab equipment.

Before leaving me to it, Vince advised me of something he said would please Cassidy should he come nosing around, "which he does from time to time": "Make one obvious mistake for him to catch and fix. Forget a zero, or leave a lid unscrewed. Don't ask me why, but he'll like you better for it."

Luis was showing me Friday's samples — 14 bottles, one from each producing well (another was off-line for repairs), when Vince returned.

"Say, Bing, why don't you take the bus out to Caldego Canyon, take a look around for yourself? Leaving in five minutes. Luis can do the tests today. Take some bound *Bulletins* with you if you want — if you can read in a car?"

"Think so."

"Good."

So I boarded a curious, canvas-topped yellow vehicle, a White Motor Co. bus retired from service in Yellowstone Park, *Pan-Hemispheric Petroleum Co.* stenciled on the side. These buses, with places for 14, shuttled back and forth all day long. Four of my fellow passengers were roughnecks, the other a cook. I didn't do much reviewing of my *Bulletins*, however, because California's scenery is so beautiful that when it unspools outside your window, you can't help but take it in. Crossing Cahuenga Pass into the Valley, we paralleled railroad tracks north, finally near Castaic turning uphill.

From miles away I could see the Caldego Canyon field, derricks pincushioning the ridge. From a distance its white-painted tank farm looked like a Mediterranean village. Pumpjacks became visible as we climbed and could take in the whole beautiful canyon.

I say beautiful; I looked at it through two sets of eyes. That one day it would be a wonderful tract for housing was obvious to the real-estate salesman in me. The topography offered varied settings for homesites with fine views, and in my mind's eye I could see how pepper and acacia trees, roses, hollyhock and bougainvillea would soften the eventual architecture, whether

Spanish in style or in the glassy modern mode the Ravens were tending towards; would produce a lushness like that of the Hollywood Hills, framing views and eluding neighbors' eyes.

But that was for the future. For now it offered an oilfield's ruined landscape, devoid of vegetation, nothing but black puddles, black mud, black scraped ground.

One road only led to Caldego Canyon's gate. We drove in past gate shack and office shack, bunkhouse and mess shack to the equipment shack, where the driver advised me to don a pair of Wellingtons against the muck.

Doing so, I embarked on a squelching solo reconnaissance. Horsehead pumps bobbed amidst half a dozen derricks. Moated with berms and ditches, the tank farm — which collected crude via pipes from the pumpjacks — stood aside with its ladders, catwalks, gangways and loading arms. The tanks were of welded steel — twelve of them, each 50,000 gallons in capacity.

My immediate impression: Those tanks represented more storage than necessary, and those derricks meant new drilling, which I confirmed by dodging out of the way of mud trucks to inspect them. Calculating in my head how much storage a field of Caldego Canyon's reported output required, I came up with a rough figure of 200,000 gallons. The tank farm in front of me would hold three times that much! Though crude would accumulate overnight, even so it represented excess capacity, given that trucks labored 12 hours a day carrying oil down to the railway where, seven days a week, trains whisked it on to the refinery.

Aside from the ever-industrious pumpjacks, the trucks were the most active things in sight. While one Kenworth carrying a 1,000-gallon tank painted *Caldego Oil Co.* was leaving after being filled up at a tank's loading arm, another would arrive for its load. Men would emerge from the pump shack, one clambering up the truck, the other the tank, and 20 minutes later it would carry off its load. At the Southern Pacific siding ten miles off I could see rail tanker cars lined up beside Caldego's bulk terminal plant for transloading. I remembered Cassidy's telling me it wouldn't pay to lay a pipeline to replace the trucks.

Having slogged my way across many acres, and introduced myself to everybody I came across, near lunchtime I knocked on the office-shack door.

It was opened by a moonfaced chap with garters holding his snowy sleeves away from his inky hands. He looked surprised to see me. Facedown on his desk was a copy of *True Detective*.

This was Mr. Browning, whom I knew to be the accountant the Ravens seconded from the Dome — their man on the spot.

Behind him, at one of the drafting tables beneath the windows, sat the on-site engineer, Mr. Spencer. He might have sensed in me a contender for *his* job, because he wasn't very friendly.

Within minutes, in a voice meant not to carry to Spencer, Browning was complaining about the mud, the dust, the noise, the smell, the roughnecks. He showed me the lunchbox he carried so he could avoid the rowdy mess shack. Clearly he missed Westwood Village's civilized confines.

He also said he avoided the company bus.

"That's my Plymouth outside," he sniffed. "Drive up from Virgil Village every day. Better that way. They may not like me, but that doesn't matter, because I'm the man with the numbers."

He showed me the ledgers spread open on the drafting tables where he collated the data Spencer gave him. Spencer toured the field daily taking samples and reading off the wells' pressure gauges and venturi flow meters.

Aside from payroll (handled by Bunker Hill) and truck upkeep (there was a garage at the siding), everything that could be counted or quantified was there in his books, Browning boasted. He seemed proudest of converting the *gallons* produced and trucked into the *barrels* of oil-industry usage (42 gallons to a barrel, he was good enough to inform me).

"Only one anomaly, but I'm following up on it."

"What's that?"

"The odometers on the Kenworths," he said. "Every truck makes six round trips a day down to the siding, for a daily total of 6,000 gallons. Twelve trucks, that's 72,000 gallons—1,715 barrels, give or take—and everything matches up.

"Except for the odometers! They're out by half! Strangest thing: It's 9.1 miles to the siding, times two for the return—18.2, follow? Multiplied by six trips a day—109.2 miles—times seven days a week: 764.4 miles a week, each truck. But week in, week out the odometers record more than 1,500 miles. I'm in correspondence with the Kenworth Motor Truck Company about it. Warned them defective odometers will make mischief in the resale market."

"Very astute, Mr. Browning," I told him.

The scale of things impressed me. At oil's recently stiffening price, Caldego Canyon was producing well over $50,000 worth of crude a month! Oil had sunk as low as 25 cents a barrel, the Depression hitting demand hard. Now it was back near a dollar, less because of any recovery in demand than from old-fashioned American price-fixing, the industry having ceded to the Texas Railroad Commission the power of setting crude's price. The Commission knew which side its bread was buttered on.

So if the Raven brothers' monthly cheques from Caldego were decreasing—well, it wasn't apparent *why*.

After Spencer went to lunch, I asked Browning about new drilling. He pointed out the window to the derricks and to where, a mile away, they were just placing the "Christmas tree" atop what he told me Cassidy had already named the *Gaisford* well. Turned out the wells had names, *Dittburner*, *Clemons*, *Propst*, etc.—all names of USC Trojans. I debated whether to inform the Ravens of the fact, which certainly showed Cassidy taking advantage.

When Browning offered me half his liverwurst sandwich, I joined the roughnecks in the mess shack for hamburgers and macaroni. Noisy but fun, and the food plentiful.

Poor Browning. He didn't persuade me that he knew what he was seeing, recording or talking about. If Cassidy was cheating his partners, Browning seemed to me unlikely to be much help in stopping him. "This business isn't like real estate," he'd complained. "I'm a fish out of water here."

Afterwards I poked around the field some more, then studied *Bulletins* while waiting for a bus back to town. Getting there at knocking-off time, I drove happily home to Pasadena.

9.

TUESDAY, THEN, WAS my first full day working in my own lab. I loved it. Luis introduced me to the routine procedures and our equipment's idiosyncrasies, and I examined samples all morning. Hours passing like minutes, at noon I was startled to find it time for lunch.

I made lunch hour a combination walk and meal. It was years since I'd been at large Downtown, and it was fun to stroll Broadway, thronged with financial types from Spring Street striding to their clubs or restaurants and with mothers in hats and white gloves taking their begloved, behatted daughters shopping at The Broadway on Fourth Street or Bullock's at Seventh.

I found my way to the brand-new Clifton's Cafeteria. Busy though it was, there was room for one more, and I carried a tray of meatloaf up to what remained my favorite refuge ever after, over the waterfall.

Returning, replete, to the office, and shrugging into my lab coat, I turned to my beakers with anticipation. My afternoon's analyses — determining the samples' sulfates through oxidative microcoulometry — soothed me. Accuracy was called for, and accuracy I happily provided.

With Vince's permission, I headed off early and drove out to Westwood to empty my desk drawer.

Walking into the Dome's hush—nothing much was going on—I startled Doreen into a smile.

"*Bing*. How nice to see you!"

She was discreetly curious about my leaving so abruptly, so we chatted as I retrieved my things. The only item I cared about was a glass paperweight with my mother's photograph embedded in it, which I slipped safely into my pocket. I couldn't tell Doreen the real reason for my transfer to Caldego Oil, of course, only said I was glad to be in the petroleum industry at last.

She told me things at the Dome continued deathly quiet.

"But we had a few lookers-in this morning, so—cross my fingers."

The Ravens, making for their waiting Cadillacs, paused to shake my hand, Mr. Thomas smiling, Mr. Delbert frowning.

"I've got a car," I told Doreen. "Like a lift home?"

"Why, sure, Bing."

We took the long way, stopping off on Hollywood Boulevard to share a hot fudge sundae at C.C. Brown's, even if it was almost dinnertime.

"They really should make you a salesman," I said.

"Meant to tell you, Bing, they *did*, just yesterday. First woman salesman, but the honor of it feels a little empty with business so flat."

"Things will pick up, Doreen. You should be proud. You'll do very well, I know it."

Rejoining the Boulevard's parade to Western Avenue, we pulled up in front of her turreted Victorian house. It had a dozen bedrooms, she told me, and most were rented out.

I wasn't angling for a dinner invitation, of course, and had spoiled my appetite anyway, but felt a little surprised when none came.

So I proposed a short walk, and we strolled up the street into

Griffith Park's Fern Dell. So lovely, those fronds overlapping one another beneath the trees; a refuge enhanced by flowing water. Arid Southern California may be, but wherever water flows— and Fern Dell catches what comes off the upper park—it's *lush*. Mediated by those fronds, daylight seeped away, transformed to the sound of tinkling water.

But what sent us scrambling was a near disaster: Hearing rustling in the underbrush, we looked over to see a skunk actually slinging its rear over its head, ready to let fly. But it didn't, apparently satisfied to see us moving smartly off.

10.

UNCLE JIM CALLED UP with Ted's invite to the Bruins' Friday night season-opener — September 27, against Utah State — and to the pep rally before the game. Telephoning Doreen, I asked her to both.

That was a happy week, thanks to my job. The work was immersive. Yes, I was new, so Vince and Luis and everybody had to show me the tasks lying within my responsibilities. I was a little chagrinned to be taken through things by my young assistant, but for the most part could give myself over to a state of concentration broken only by a lunch hour that seemed to come out of nowhere and then, more forcibly, by the rush for the exits at 5:00 o'clock. Lovely.

In addition to analyzing daily samples — the repaired *Warburton* well came back on line that week — I helped work up paperwork with a view to the end-of-month reports to be filed with the State, tabulating totals, figuring averages, plotting trends. Great fun.

Friday afternoon, I picked up Doreen at the Dome and we went on to UCLA and parked at the oval below the Janss Steps. Climbing them, we marveled as we achieved the level of the quadrangle's stately new buildings. Of course, being so new, the campus lacked the ivy or the trees upholding a canopy of a really hallowed one; it looked rather stark.

We met Jim, Ted and Miss Raven at the end of the bridge
across the ravine, Jim having driven out of his way to spare Ted
extra steps. Minus six-shooter or star, but wearing his Stetson
and gabardine shirt, he looked like an overaged rodeo rider.

Even so, escorting my cousin across to the Men's
Gymnasium to suit up seemed an event torn from the pages of a
fairy tale. Co-eds squealed at the sight of Ted shambling along
in sleepy river-god mode, and men called, "Hey, Ted, how's it
going?" or "Go Bruins!" Ted's smile was wide and easy as he
lobbed back greetings or stopped to autograph books and
programs.

Arriving at the gym at the head of a crowd, Ted went up two
steps, turned around, raised his hands, shouted, "See you all at
the game!" and *sprinted* into the building. It tore a roar from our
throats; we looked at one another as though something
significant had passed through our lives.

Meanwhile students, scholars, rooters and boosters were
converging—the published estimate was *4,000*—to support and
celebrate their Bruins: underclassmen in dinks, coeds in pleated
skirts and cardigans, upperclassmen, faculty, administrators, the
men who wrote the cheques, everyone cheering as the marching
band emerged blaring from Royce Hall's arcade and
cheerleaders sprang up in astonishing formations.

When the music stopped, UCLA's Dean of Men, Earl G.
Miller, delivered a peroration from the steps. If a little flat, it was
well received; Miller was beloved ever since he paid out of his
own pocket for the broken windows from the snowball fight
of 1932.

Then Coach Spaulding told us how proud of his boys he was;
Utah State wouldn't know what hit 'em! He introduced his
starting eleven and their backups in a choreographed pageant of
flying footballs and players jogging in place, propelled by drums
whose thumps and beats penetrated us and echoed off walls,

while lurid brass lines stirred our blood. The quadrangle roared!

Had to admit, it was a team of bruisers—but none more menacing than Texas Ted. Ordinarily a handsome guy with a friendly expression, when looking out from the line of scrimmage, or being photographed in uniform, or posing at a pep rally, Ted had a trick of wrinkling his nose and curling his lip in a way that pulled his chin up and hairline down, making his face a grotesque mask that had even the curl at his widow's peak look like it was coming for you.

Surely that was the face of a man with murder in his heart? *Hooray!*

Doreen loved it; so did Miss Raven. And if not swept up in the hysteria—carried out of himself by drums and trumpets— Uncle Jim enjoyed it, too.

After final drumming crescendos, it was on to the Coliseum! Doreen and I joined the torchlight parade down to Wilshire Boulevard (dusk sufficiently advanced to lend it some credence), where most boarded the waiting buses, and we returned to my car.

Driving to the Coliseum we were silent. Feelings are something I'm not very good at. I was excited—had to be after that rally—but quiet. That Doreen, too, was subdued told me how comfortable with each other we were.

Well.

After parking on the Ravens' reserved patch of tarmac (a great privilege), we streamed in with other fans, the UCLA students among us wearing the required blue-and-gold rooting caps. Soon we were in the bleachers next to Uncle Jim, just yards from the field. Floodlights aimed from high stanchions rendered the gridiron's green fantastical and glamorous, while leaving us spectators swallowed up in darkness.

Despite possibly the whole student body attending, swelling the crowd of spectators to more than 12,000, the enormous bowl — built for eight times that many — seemed empty. For one night only the Coliseum was dubbed *the Mausoleum*.

Mr. Thomas turned and waved me over to where he sat between his daughter and brother.

"So how's the job going, Bing?"

"Challenging, Mr. Raven, but I like it."

"Find anything yet?" I was startled, and must have shown it, because he laughed. "That's OK, you just started."

As the game began, the yell leaders — who'd handed out megaphones to those of us in the cheer sections — led us in chants with the inimitable Joe E. Brown's assistance. It being too dark for the usual halftime card stunts, they also distributed flashlights with colored lenses for a first-ever attempt at "light stunts;" judging by the response from across the way, a success!

And what a game! I'd attended some at OSU, always in the nosebleed sections where the action seemed at a remove. No escaping it at the 50-yard line! Not only could I hear thumps of flesh against flesh, leather against leather, but every groan, grunt and cry of pain from the players, while Coach Spaulding bawled, *"Turn it on! D'ye think we're washing dishes?"*

Utah State never stood a chance. The Bruins were on fire, Texas Ted flaming brightest of all in the first quarter. He scored the first touchdown, bulling through the defensive line and dashing 25 yards, our souls flying along with him in ecstatic release. Punching through their defenses, he was sometimes slowed but seldom stopped. When he *was* buried, it was heart-stopping to see players unpeel themselves from on top of him, see him get up and limp to the sidelines. But always he returned, until in the second quarter Coach took out his starters and put in the second, then third, then fourth teams. It was a slaughter, 39-0!

Before we parted that evening, Uncle Jim invited Doreen and me to brunch at the Ravens' next day.

First he had to explain to me what "brunch" is.

"Bring an appetite," he added. "Mr. Delbert puts on quite a spread."

11.

THE NEXT MORNING, the desiccated look of the hills lending a hint of fall to what felt like a summer's day, I trekked out to Holmby Hills.

But first I picked up Doreen. Her maid admitted me to a stair hall of mahogany columns with a carpeted staircase and pocket doors open to the parlor, and called to a buxom, kindly woman coming down the steps — Doreen's mother. It was a finer house than I'd expected, if old-fashioned in its dark woodwork and red-velvet draperies.

Exclaiming at her daughter's sudden interest in football — "Doreen so enjoyed the game!" — Mrs. Vorhees dispatched the maid upstairs to fetch her. The house was quiet; no one was stirring. Apparently her boarders were sleeping in, knackered from their week's auditions or work as movie extras.

And there came Doreen down the stairs. We got going through the delicious morning.

Seeing me breathe deep as we drove down Western Avenue, she remarked, "I always think the air in Los Angeles is like champagne, don't you?"

"Never had it," I said.

"Never had *champagne?* We'll have to fix that! What I mean is it's bubbly, tickles your nose, makes you happy."

"Not like Ohio's, I'll give it that."

Soon, wheeling through the gates on Sunset, I was saluting the guard and Doreen gasping as Mr. Thomas's house came into view. Her first time there.

We took the turning to Uncle Jim's. He came out in a rawhide jacket, fringes front and back, sporting his biggest silver belt buckle.

"Come on, getting the whole team over to Mr. Delbert's," he said, putting on his Stetson. Over his shoulder he called, "Ted, you ready?"

And here came Texas Ted, grinning, if clearly in some pain. I introduced Doreen and he told me, "Got yourself a white leghorn for sure." High praise indeed.

At his hobbling pace we took the path next door. By the time we reached Mr. Delbert's and crossed the lawn to the terrace set out with tables and umbrellas and filling up with his teammates, Ted had warmed up some, the limping less noticeable as he called greetings to pals and coaches.

While a troupe of servants carried dishes to tables at the side, removing covers to reveal steaming steaks, eggs, bacon, sausages, biscuits, muffins and grits, the Raven brothers beamed at their enormous, slope-shouldered, muscular guests.

Mr. Delbert demanded everybody's attention.

"Terrific game last night. *Kudos* to Coach Spaulding and all of you. Texas Ted, you were a standout! Made us very proud!"

To yells and clapping, Ted did his best aw-shucks dip of the head.

"All right, fellows, get your food and eat up all you like!"

Winking, Mr. Thomas added, "There's orange juice, tomato juice and coffee, and if you want 'em fortified, just say the word."

We found food and a shady table. Not sure what was in bloom, but it smelled as good as the food tasted.

Finished eating, some took up Mr. Thomas's invitation to

find bathing suits in his pool house next door. Games of doubles started on Mr. Delbert's tennis courts, and games of croquet and badminton on the lawn. Very jolly.

Doreen nudging me, I looked up to see Mr. Delbert wagging his finger. I followed him indoors, passing between linebackers flanking the door like caryatids who carried on talking right over my head. Humbling to be among such giants.

Darker inside than his brother's, his house, too, was modeled on some English manor from the time of Henry VIII or so. Passing through anterooms and French doors, Mr. Delbert led me into a lofty space with balconies at either end.

"Have a seat, Bing. Glad of a chance to catch up."

He smiled as we sat down. His smile was a professional job — as a homebuilder and trustee of UCLA, he always had one at the ready, correct in form and contour and very like a real one, too, except the eyes were missing from it.

Made my skin crawl a bit.

"How're they treating you at Caldego Oil?"

"Fine, Mr. Raven. Getting into the routine of analyzing samples."

"Those samples, are they real?"

I was startled. "Why wouldn't they be?"

"What, they come in bottles labeled 'Caldego Well No. 7,' do they?"

"Exactly —"

"Bing, Bing, Bing: You need to fill the bottles *yourself*, seal them up *yourself*."

"You suspect the *samples* are —?"

"The sleeper awakens!"

I heard distant Bruin squeals of joy, and crows cawing.

"All right, Mr. Raven, I'll go out and bottle some myself. What comes from a given well's usually about the same — wells have their signatures, you know. We graph the gravity, viscosity, sulfur content, like that, so I'll see how my samples match up with what they've been giving me. Yes, that's the way to do it. Knew you wanted to keep tabs—not that you were so suspicious."

"You don't know with whom we're dealing. Well, good. And count the wells while you're at it—and derricks and pumpjacks, everything. By the way, any idea the size of next month's cheque?"

"No, sir: Different division. The accountants follow the oil to point of sale—"

He slapped his knees and stood up.

"Let's get back to the party."

12.

DESPITE WHAT I TOLD Mr. Delbert, I didn't go out to the field that week. A swift perusal of records Monday morning showed that my recent analyses lined up with those going back to the drilling of each well, making a trip to Caldego Canyon futile.

More important—not that I was swift enough to remember it while talking with him—in a financial sense any variations in crude didn't amount to a hill of beans. No, if Cassidy was cheating his partners, it wasn't by doctoring samples, but by fudging the volumes shipped, and I couldn't imagine how he might manage *that*. Anyway, with my end-of-month reports to see to, followed by routine start-of-month procedures, I didn't go anywhere.

Except for an excursion one day that week, when Vince put me on the bus to take a look at the refinery. I was willing.

Partway to Long Beach, we passed in the freshness of the morning the most out-of-the-world thing I ever saw: structures like iron armatures for a cathedral's bell towers and, attached to them, glistening in the sun—*dinner plates? Glass?* A man silhouetted near the top of one was welding rebar to it in a cascade of sparks. The Watts Towers have since become famous. I didn't know then what to make of them, nor do I now.

But Pan-Hemispheric's refinery was every bit as abstract as the Watts Towers—shiny thermal cracking units, bubble towers and vacuum distillation columns, all state-of-the-art modern. Crude oil from Cassidy's different fields was pumped through various processes to produce the gasoline, kerosene, diesel fuel and heating oil that Pan-Hemispheric sold throughout the West. Everything smelled of petroleum, was coated in petroleum, slippery with petroleum and the roar was incessant: *Marvelous!* If the Watts Towers were one man's cracked dream, the refinery expressed civilization's choice to master its environment.

Mac, the chief, was expecting me, and gave me the grand tour—handed me Wellingtons, mackintosh and hard hat, and led me through the complex from the highest flare platform down to where railroad tanker cars obediently stepped forward to be emptied of crude or filled with gasoline. At one time the site must have been an attractive residential quarter, for the offices were housed in a left-over Victorian manse set in a landscape of pipes. With a pang I thought of Violet's family home.

It was a lot to take in, as I told Mac over lunch. We were gathered in the manse's dining room, a hearty repast in front of us, when—as happens in the oil game—a call came in. Placing napkins over our plates, we hurried out to solve the crisis.

This one arose in a new operation where they wished to produce petcoke. Having installed four reactors made of high-temperature steel, they were carbonizing char in the first one using flue gases, partially activating it with steam in the second, drying it in the third. But dropping it into reactor #4 was failing—despite *its* steam—to deposit carbon on the base char.

No one knew what to do. Half a dozen supervisors—one of them just promoted from doing my job Downtown—were standing around scratching their heads, upset at the possible loss of a large expenditure, when I suggested impregnating the third reactor's char with a solution of metal salts.

They scoffed—all but Mac, who thought about it and

nodded. They tried it and it worked: Soon they had their petcoke. Which, in turn, worked a marvelous change in their estimation of *me*.

"Might be something to that book-learning of yours," Mac allowed as we returned to our cold, cold lunch.

Very nice day. In Watts as the bus returned Downtown late afternoon's rich sunshine enveloped that same solitary spider, enmeshed in his web as he attached bits of china to the structure. Sparkling in the sun, they looked like birds singing in trees.

I suppose it's a great nation that can accommodate the occasional loose screw spending his days so unproductively, when mine had given me the satisfaction of helping make people their fuel.

FOR THAT WEEK'S GAME against Oregon State in Portland, the Ravens chartered special cars that, coupled to the Sunset Limited, carried hundreds north. Alas, I wasn't able to join them.

But Uncle Jim invited me over to hear it on KEJK. An occasional pipe smoker, he filled his meerschaum as we sat on his veranda listening to the radio and looking out at Mr. Thomas's gables and chimneys poking up over the hedge.

It was a suspenseful game. Oregon State scored early, the Bruins not until the fourth quarter, when their "machine-gunners" (per the *Times)* finally came into play. What a quarter! Jim took out his pipe and chortled when the announcer yelled, "And *Texas Ted* punches out the first down on Oregon State's 42!" The Bruins scoring, Ted set up to kick the extra point. I held my breath, knowing he'd foozled it under the cross-arm the year before, but: "*Groves* place-kicks the extra point, and — *holy cow!* — that ball's cleared the wall of Multnomah Stadium!"

UCLA took it, 20-7. "Helluva player, that boy," Jim allowed.

But what occurred next was scandalous. All the papers had

it: When their bespoke train returned to Glendale's Southern Pacific depot Sunday afternoon, no one was there to meet it, except for Uncle Jim, me and other family members. Where was the Dean of Men? Where the student-body president—not to mention the student body? Not even a photographer, much less a newsreel crew! Like mere mortals our victors had to lug their own bags out to the parking lot.

It's never happened again.

Last of all came Ted, grinning as he picked his way, at every step going "*Ow.*" At least I was able to take his suitcase. He got in the car saying softly, "*Ow – ow – ow.*"

"Just take your time, son," Jim told him.

13.

I INVITED DOREEN TO ACCOMPANY ME to Palo Alto for the Bruins' next game, after a bye week, against the Stanford Indians; when she accepted, I bought seats on the Bruin Special. We would spend two nights on the train, coming and going. Heroic efforts were afoot to get rooters and boosters north, especially via auto convoys carrying *thousands*.

That week I'd finally made my promised visit to Caldego Canyon, and duly filled bottles at each pumpjack's stopcock. Back at the lab, I confirmed that their contents aligned with those of previous samples, and left word to that effect with Mr. Delbert's secretary—glad not to have to inform him personally about that disappointing result.

At the pep rally before our departure—the campus cry all week being, *"On to Stanford!"*—the air was autumnally thin, so expansive as to carry our roars across the sky. The *Daily Bruin* proclaimed, "The hills of Westwood rang again!"

Then occurred an amazing nighttime procession led by buses filled with every member of the team, their coaches, managers, porters and physicians, the band, cheerleaders and yell leaders, plus *400 cars*—flivvers to limousines—with police cruisers and motorcycles, fire engines and ambulances, every vehicle decked out with blue-and-gold streamers and moving in an earsplitting cacophony of horns and sirens as, ignoring stoplights, we roared up Sunset, down Hollywood, up Los Feliz and Riverside to Glendale, streamers snapping in the air.

What a glorious sight!

Inevitably the crush at the depot resulted in delaying the Sunset Limited's 8:00 p.m. departure, but what did it matter? Doreen with her little marble suitcase, I with my leather one, we thanked our driver, merrily showed our blue-and-gold tickets (expensive, but worth it!) and boarded. Ours was the last seat in our car, so amidst chants and cheers and streamers trailing down the aisle, we found ourselves in effect alone with each other until the berths were made up. Just as we wished to be.

Pulling into San Francisco the next morning we were a little fatigued. Buses took us to the Palace Hotel at Market and New Montgomery Streets. Luggage stayed on the train, for the return trip was to start after that evening's dinner-dance, but rooms were reserved for our daytime convenience, too.

At the splendid breakfast provided, Doreen and I were seated at a table with two men in rooter jackets who could talk nothing but Bruins. Mischievously — but I forgave her — Doreen let drop that I was cousin to Texas Ted, and the onslaught of questions never stopped. When, as we stepped away, I murmured that it wouldn't surprise me if our companions stole the cutlery hallowed by being used by Texas Ted's own cousin, Doreen looked back and confirmed they were doing exactly that.

Finding that you share a sense of humor with someone is to make a real advance, I think.

Afterwards we walked up hill and down. Neither of us had been to Frisco in years, so that bright morning was great fun. How one likes to see a city gives another clue about compatibility. Most of our fellows venturing no farther than the stores on Union Square, I felt lucky to be with someone willing to scout out the loftiest views and lowest wharfsides.

After lunch, we took the special train to Stanford's stadium, crowded with 25,000 people, where our contingent raised quite a ruckus – until the other 20,000 deigned to drown us out.

Bands blared and marched, an invocation came over the scratchy P.A., the teams took the field, a coin was tossed and the game that some still call UCLA's *best ever* began.

It was a fight for the ages.

Stanford, defending PCC champion and undefeated, had a fearsome nickname: *The Vow Boys* (the vow being never to lose to USC). The Vow Boys intercepted early and succeeded in running the ball over the goal line: 6-0; but they missed the extra point. Soon, "Moosenose" Cheshire scooped up Stanford's fumble and he and Texas Ted began running the ball towards the goal. After a struggle, in two 7-yard plunges Ted got it across: *Touchdown!* 6-6: tie game!

Then Texas Ted kicked the extra point: 6-7, UCLA!

All this in the first quarter. From that point the game ground on, and on, and on, both sides' heroic efforts unavailing, each under threat by the other every moment. Terrific suspense and strain.

UCLA's yearbook later remarked,

> The scoreboard tells but little of the brilliant battle. The timber of the goal posts proved of far weaker stuff than that which gave the Bruin squad the will to win.

Stanford drove 253 yards to UCLA's 75, had 16 first downs to UCLA's 2, but never scored again. Every mighty *crunch!* of lines crashing into each other gave way to the next *crunch!* but the end zones remained unvisited. Meanwhile, Joe E. Brown led us in yells he composed for the occasion.

When the game finally ended – the score still 6-7 – we huzza'd ourselves hoarse. A horde of our fans ran onto the field and smashed Stanford's goal posts to splinters! The Ravens were ecstatic: Their Bruins were poised for the PCC championship and the Rose Bowl, and Texas Ted, having scored every point for

UCLA, had *All-American* in the bag.

Taking the happy train back to the hotel, we found the Rose Room — for the night renamed the Rose *Bowl* Room — resplendent in blue and gold, and we dined and danced to *Paul Pendarvis and His UCLA Orchestra*. For the first time I held Doreen in my arms. After taking advantage of the garden for a few liberties near the close of the evening, we boarded the bus for the depot and our 1:30 a.m. departure.

Despite the victory, the trip home was subdued, everybody being exhausted. Shortly after I retired to my lower berth, some fraternity youngsters installed their drunken fellow in the upper, positioning a basin at his head in case of need. Fortunately, he fell asleep without incident.

Doreen and I met up in the dining car for breakfast and sat together afterwards. Pulling into Glendale about noontime, we were greeted by a cavalcade of streamer-bedecked vehicles. Our players emerged from their sleeping car to cheers, and his teammates helped Ted down the long step to the platform. He moved painfully, but looked happy and fulfilled: *The man who won the game.*

Horns and sirens kept up the din going back to campus.

Our driver let Doreen off at her corner, and she insisted I come inside for Sunday lunch. Mrs. Vorhees, if startled, kindly welcomed me.

We ate in a fine dining room with stained-glass windows, on the table very acceptable baked chicken. The boarders — young women, most of them blonde and quite beautiful — joined us, straggling in yawning. Something I found curious (but of course didn't remark on) was that while we had lunch, the boarders ate breakfast, and also that they said scarcely anything, although they appeared to find me humorous. At least, I guessed that to be the purport of their arching their eyebrows at one another.

I'd never asked Doreen about her father — sometimes that's a minefield, especially in a town like Hollywood. But there at table she volunteered that at the moment Papa was "in the field." It developed that he was a prospector. Seems his parents took him as a boy to visit Sutter's Mill, where—plunging his hands into the riverside muck—he came up with a small but indubitable gold nugget and knew right away what he wanted to do with his life.

He'd pursued gold now for 30 years. It was a hard life of trekking deserts, climbing mountains and wading glacial streams, but finally, ten years earlier, he'd made his strike, hitting a vein in the Sierra Nevadas and opening a mine—the *Doreen*—that yielded some 1,000 ounces of gold.

But even as he was planning to extend the mine, his wife swooped in and spent part of his proceeds buying the boarding house that had sustained her and her daughter ever since.

"So at least we have a roof over our heads," said Doreen.

"Very smart."

"Before we had this house, Papa wasn't above putting us up in ghost-town shacks where, if we wanted to eat, Mother had to go out and shoot a rabbit."

"Lordy."

"But you'd like him, Bing, even if he *is* a bit touched."

"I'm sure I would."

14.

SUNDAY'S *TIMES* HEADLINE was:

BRUINS BLAST STANFORD
"TEXAS TED" SCORES ALL OF U.C.L.A.'s POINTS, HANDS INDIAN TITLE HOPES TERRIFIC SETBACK

One halftone photograph caught Ted barreling through Stanford's line, a cannonball of fury, body hunched over the ball, leg kicked outwards, *flying*. Another showed the winning kick, his leg high as a ballerina's, breathtaking in its extension and grace. In that era, football players wore thin padding and leather helmets without faceguards, and looked vulnerable and human, unlike the stylized figures of the present-day game.

The story noted,

> In two overpowering smashes, Groves was over for the Bruins' score, and followed up his brilliant line-lunging by kicking goal.

The next game was the big one on October 26: UCLA *vs.* USC, with its 2-2 record. "The most anticipated game of the year," the *Times* called it, noting Bing Crosby's fruitless attempt to be released from his contract for the weekend that he might attend. I was looking forward to it myself.

On Thursday evening, Doreen telephoned to say that Cassidy had come by the Dome that day with the Ravens' monthly Caldego Oil cheque, this one for just less than $8,000 – another drop.

She told me that when Mr. Delbert expressed surprise at the cheque's size, since the price of oil was up a nickel, Cassidy allowed as how, yes, thank goodness oil was up, because the Caldego Canyon field seemed to him about played out. Then they'd joshed about their bet on the coming match-up of Bruins *vs.* Trojans.

"After he left, the Ravens had an argument in Mr. Delbert's office," she said. "Lots of shouting, and when they came out Mr. Delbert told me – *asked* me – to remind you they're counting on you, Bing. Do you know what he means?"

Yes, I did. At least I had the wit to ask her to the game. She accepted, and went me one better, having cadged invitations to the team's game-day breakfast – an exclusive booster affair. And after breakfast we would "brunch" at the home of a friend she wished me to meet.

I hung up excited – if fretful about Caldego Canyon. Perhaps I had better get out there again?

I did it the next day, though it meant missing the season's biggest pep rally. Again I donned Wellingtons, squelched around everywhere and looked in on Browning. He seemed glad to have someone to talk to. Counting men, wells and two new derricks near the field's northern end, again I wondered: Why drill in a supposedly dying field?

After lunch I hitched a ride with a tanker driver down to Caldego's bulk terminal plant at the railway siding, next to the garage and truck yard. It had a row of huge horizontal tanks, their capacity easily twice what was needed. A pumpman fitted his loading arm's hose to the Kenworth's manhole, switched on his pump, and it was just a matter of waiting as it pumped its haul into the tanks. Meanwhile, another pumpman was loading crude from those tanks into tanker cars. I walked the length of the train: 20 cars of some 7,500 gallons capacity apiece. That the daily train had enough cars to carry *twice* our daily production seemed a puzzling waste.

I rode back up to Caldego Canyon with the same taciturn driver who'd taken me down to the railway. (I might add, on both trips his odometer appeared to work fine.) He drove the Kenworth to the tank farm, where another truck was being loaded, and honked. Two men came out of the pump shack to attend to him. One climbed to the tank's loading arm and swiveled it over the truck. The other fitted the hose's nozzle atop the Kenworth and yanked the chain; crude gushed and gurgled into its tank. It didn't take long. When the tank was full, the pumpmen detached the hose, closed the manhole, rapped the Kenworth and off it drove.

I introduced myself to the pumpmen, telling them I worked Downtown for Mr. Cassidy, and they welcomed me inside their shack and poured me coffee. They had a cook stove, cots, a bookcase filled with notebooks and, on the table, face-down hands of cards, which now they picked up.

Ray and Roy were brothers. They explained how they fed trucks 12 hours a day, and quite liked it, confiding that it involved little actual *labor* and gave them plenty of time for playing euchre, hearts, gin rummy and poker with each other and the other team of pumpmen, and sometimes double solitaire with waiting truck drivers.

"Imagine you keep records of the trucks you fill?" I asked.

"You bet," said Ray, indicating the bookcase while, with a crafty smile at Roy, he played a card. "Every week, send them over to Mr. Browning."

"Mind if I take a look?"

"Knock yourself out," he said. "More coffee?"

I sat down with a fresh cup as the other team came indoors, even as another Kenworth honked and the brothers went out to tend to it. But I was disappointed: Their records matched up with Browning's and ours Downtown. If discrepancies there were, they weren't to be found in the pumphouse records.

Did I have to tell the Ravens they were barking up the wrong tree?

Their Kenworth loaded and headed for the siding, Ray and Roy came back indoors and, after jotting down its number, load, the date and time of day, resumed their card game.

Needing the outhouse, I found the odorous booth near by and aimed my high-pressure stream at its hole. But watching it vanish gave me a brainstorm.

What was it Professor Waldrop tried to pound into my head year after year in Columbus? *"Never assume!"*

I'd been poking about *assuming* that the figures given me were based on coaxing Caldego Canyon's crude oil out of the ground at the fastest rate possible. A well's rate of flow depends on its wellhead pressure. Now I suddenly realized that I should be able to calculate those wellhead pressures *myself,* and thus be able to double-check the accuracy of all the other figures given me — barrels produced, truckloads of oil, etc. — and not have to *assume* anything.

Buttoning up, I went back inside.

"What can you gentlemen tell me about wellhead pressures?"

"Nothing to do with us," said Roy.

Ray specified, "Mr. Browning would have those logs."

I thanked them and headed for the office shack.

When I asked Browning — "Oh, you mean the borehole logs?" — he readily lifted an oversized tome onto a drafting table.

"Hope you can read it," he said. "Greek to me."

Fascinating document, recording its data not in words but in engineering language: Spencer drew a daily wireline log for each well, comprising data for pore pressures, deviation surveys, viscosities and chlorides, and so on. Their multi-colored lines beside lists of figures made for eloquent peaks and valleys.

I pulled out my trusty brass-and-ivory slide rule and, concentrating on the borehole log for Well No. 7, the *Pappas*, calculated how many barrels a day it should give us, given its wireline log data and the natural flow, gravity, mud-weight, the pumpjack's pipe diameter and power, the settings of the pipe ram.

And *lo and behold!* My slide rule proved that the *Pappas* should produce *400* barrels of crude a day. So decreed the Laws of Physics! But Browning's records had it actually pumping but *200*.

And so with the others, according to my preliminary clicking of ivory over brass: Each well was capable of pumping something like *twice* its official rate of production. Why was Cassidy taking from Caldego Canyon but *half* the oil it wanted to give him? I was perplexed.

"This is all very interesting, Mr. Browning. Thank you."

"Oh, you are most welcome."

I headed to the mess shack, where Cookie poured me more coffee while I waited for the next bus back to town.

Its driver kindly stopped off at a Pan-Hemispheric service station in Burbank; I couldn't hold out a moment longer.

15.

AFTER DINNER THAT EVENING, I telephoned Uncle Jim both to ask directions to the team breakfast and to wonder out loud to a receptive pair of ears why Cassidy appeared to be leaving so much oil in the ground at Caldego Canyon.

"Isn't that like leaving money on the table?" he asked.

"Exactly!"

"*Hmm*, doesn't hardly seem Cassidy's style. How's that fit in with the truck odometers?"

"Have to give that some thought," I said shortly, not wishing to be drawn into Browning's obsession.

"Think I'll take a drive out there, Doc, take a look for myself," Jim drawled. "Care to join me?"

"What, *tonight?* It's all closed up!"

"Can swing by, pick you up on the way."

"All right, Jim, if you're going anyway."

Within the hour he pulled up in front of the house and I hurried out.

Like himself, his vehicle was a bit embarrassing, being a Model A Ford the same vintage as mine, but customized somewhere along the way, the back of the roof cut off (apparently with a can opener) and backseat replaced by a truck bed, a wood-framed window at our shoulders, and the whole thing unfortunately painted white. Jim said he'd bought it off a milkman. We'd have looked like a couple of Okies, except, thankfully, it was night.

But it did have a manifold heater. Had to keep our feet off the firewall, and the cab smelled of fumes, but at least we were toasty in the night chill.

And it drove fine. Jim had me take the wheel. It was a dark drive even before leaving the city—Los Angeles has always skimped on streetlights—and a long one, and Uncle Jim a less than chatty companion, except for filling me in about the "doozy" of a pep rally I'd missed: "Real humdinger, Doc."

We took it out past La Cañada Flintridge to the railroad, which we followed towards Castaic, at Caldego Oil's bulk terminal plant—all lit up, though the daily train had long since departed—turning uphill.

As we approached Caldego Canyon, we could see uncanny flares of natural gas burning at choke lines throughout the field. Invisible by day, they illuminated the night sky.

Headlights came towards us.

"What's this?" asked Jim as a Kenworth passed.

"Don't know," I answered.

We soon caught up with the taillights of another tanker lumbering up to the oilfield and let it lead the way. As it rolled through the fence past the gate shack, we parked to watch. The man closing the gate—firmly, with a clank—looked at us suspiciously.

Drilling was taking place a mile off, where I'd seen new wells going in. Swarms of roughnecks attended the derricks, and we could hear distant metallic booms and the rhythmic ticking of drill strings being fed into holes or pulled from them—brutal, forceful sounds amplified by the still night air and infernally lighted by gas flares and electric lights. The mess shack was open, and the office shack, too, where someone—not Spencer—was sitting at Spencer's post marking up logs: They had a night engineer, though no sign of a night bookkeeper.

That drilling was taking place at night didn't much surprise me; with some wells, goring the dragon underground requires around-the-clock efforts. But that the tank farm was also active, the loading arms lit up and a pair of pumpmen setting about filling the Kenworth we'd followed uphill even as another, already loaded, nosed its way towards us, *was* a surprise.

After a long while, Jim said, "Well, shut my mouth, Doc. See what I'm seeing?"

"Dammit, Jim, makes me feel stupid. They've got a whole night shift going!"

"Don't feel bad, you cracked the case. You're a good detective, Doc: We've got the bastard now. Got him!"

He smiled as though he'd soon be meting out some true Texas justice.

"*Stupid, stupid, stupid.* Jim, how'd you figure it out?"

"Just a suspicious old coot, I guess, Doc."

When our laden tanker came out the gate again we trailed it down the hill, 1,000 gallons of Caldego Canyon crude that only Cassidy would profit from; the Ravens weren't to know about it.

The truck pulling into the terminal, I drove us back to Pasadena, and poor weary Jim drove on home.

First, pondering how to let the Ravens know, we decided to tell them at the team breakfast.

"You go ahead, Uncle Jim. You deserve the credit."

"Don't care about credit. Get some sleep."

16.

OCTOBER 26 WAS A GLORIOUS SATURDAY. Seven years in Ohio had renewed my appreciation for Southern California's climate, and that October was just as sweet a month as you could wish for, and that Saturday perhaps its prettiest day. I loved it despite being tired from our nocturnal field trip.

Don't know what it was that perfumed the air, but something's always in bloom.

I picked up Doreen and we drove on to the Beverly Hills Hotel — in those days not pink, but still a bright white — for that's where the Ravens put up the Bruins before home games.

Great fun. Found Ted in fine river-god form. He insisted on our sitting next to him and his dad. Who seemed so creaky the previous weekend was easy, relaxed, graceful as he plied himself with orange juice and beefsteak and made eyes at Miss Raven, sitting across the floor with her father and uncle. It was fun to be in his glamorous glow, and although some food was thrown during the course of the meal, none touched him, or us.

"Hope you can come to my birthday party?" he asked us. "Friday, at Mr. Thomas's pool? There'll be cake and ice cream."

"Sure thing," I replied. "Thanks."

Doreen asked, "How old are you going to be, Ted?"

"Twenty-one," he answered, holding her eyes while Jim assiduously chewed sausage. "I'm a junior."

182

Twenty-six, more like, I thought, but didn't say it. Brushing the curl off his forehead, Ted changed the subject.

"Say, Bing, I'm in Professor Lily B. Campbell's Shakespeare class? And what fun! Me, liking *Henry the Fifth?* Has us read out loud, and she says my Prince Hal's not half bad!

> *"The southern wind*
> *Doth play the trumpet to his purposes,*
> *And by his hollow whistling in the leaves*
> *Foretells a tempest and a blust'ring day."*

"Knew it," I said. "You're going to end up in pictures."

He flashed a grin. After all, John Wayne had been a tackle at USC.

Big day for him and his teammates, facing their arch-nemesis, but they seemed confident. Myself, I thought game and wager safe, though when it comes to the game of football you never know what might happen.

After the Ravens cleared their plates, Jim gave me the high sign and we went over. Saying we had something they'd want to hear, Jim asked if there were someplace private we could go.

Exchanging looks of concern, they came to their feet and led us to an adjoining room. There Jim indicated I should go ahead.

"Jim and I have discovered that Cassidy's sure enough cheating you," I started, "and how he's doing it."

"*The hell you say?*" they responded in unison like a vaudeville act, faces flushing.

"By day, they log everything that goes on at Caldego Canyon — meticulously — and Cassidy apparently pays you according to what's logged.

"But those logs are only *half* complete — just *half* the story. The wellhead pressures prove, for instance, that the *Pappas* well — By the way, did you know Cassidy names the wells for Trojans?"

"Tell them about the night shift," Jim prompted.

"The *night* shift?" exclaimed Mr. Delbert, Mr. Thomas

echoing, *"Night* shift?"

"They pump and ship all night long, in at least the same volumes as by day, but keeping no records," I said, with possibly misplaced enthusiasm. "Well, the railroad must have records, but—"

"Bastard!" Mr. Thomas said, and Mr. Delbert: "The *bastard!"*

"Jim and I went out there last night and saw them, and anyone who knows what he's reading could see what the borehole logs imply."

"State Oil and Gas Commission?"

"They'll be fascinated, because they're getting paid only half the tax they're owed. Uncle Sam might be interested, too."

"You've got him now," Uncle Jim said. "Doc's a real detective."

"Keep this to yourselves," advised Mr. Delbert.

"For *now,"* Mr. Thomas said, "but we want you at the Dome when he pays off the bet."

"Dome if we win," his brother put in. "Pan-Hemispheric if we lose."

Added Mr. Thomas, "Explains the damn odometers."

We returned to the dining room. I was feeling good as players began to drift away and, under benevolent booster eyes, board buses hung with blue-and-gold bunting. Doreen and I wished Ted luck as he wiped his mouth and sauntered after his teammates in his energy-conserving way.

We lingered over coffee, finding the quiet of the emptied-out room pleasant after the gridders' boisterousness. Then it was on to the next event of our crowded social calendar, brunch at Doreen's Hollywood friend's.

It developed that she and Aline Barnsdall knew each other through their fathers; Miss Barnsdall's also had scouted the West for years, though chasing after oil, not gold. Finally succeeding in Oklahoma, he built a refinery in a little burg he conveniently named for himself. Doreen thought it wouldn't come amiss for me to meet a refinery owner.

She directed my Model A along Sunset to the foot of a conical hill rising from the Hollywood flats, and up a driveway that spiraled through lush plantings. The drive was walled with concrete blocks impressed with a hollyhock motif, and at one turning cottages built of similar blocks were poised above the view. At the top we came to a wide, level lawn embraced by a pavilion of concrete block and glass.

"Aline calls it Hollyhock House," Doreen said. "You've never seen anything like it."

Nor had I. Almost disorienting in its effect, the house wrapped us not in boxes within boxes, but in spaces that flowed according to programs of light and air; not *completely* strange to me at that, for I sensed a relation to Dad's Greene Brothers house. The architect was one Frank Lloyd Wright.

A tall, amused-looking lady resplendent in silver-and-turquoise Indian jewelry and a pleated silk gown by (Doreen told me) Fortuny welcomed us and directed us to buffet tables, from whose offerings—after our beefsteak breakfast—we chose sparingly. Doreen was delighted to find the butler pouring flutes of champagne, so at last I had my first nose-tickling taste of it (not for me, I'm afraid).

I found myself trying to answer our hostess's questions about my degrees and ambitions and whether I liked Oklahoma.

Told her I'd never been.

"You'd love it, Bing," she said. "Good place for someone like you. Dad's refinery makes more wax than any in the world—supplies Johnson Wax and the others.

"Really?" I said, perking up. "My dissertation was on—"

"*Mona!*" gushed our hostess to a new arrival who looked vaguely familiar—a movie actress. "*Lovely* to see you."

17.

BY 2:15 – GAME TIME – Doreen and I were nestled at the Coliseum's 50-year-line, among the 74,878 souls that had gathered, minus the not-yet-arrived Ravens and Uncle Jim and whoever had the stretch of empty bleacher just across the aisle.

But those particular seats filled up when, like a mother goose, a matronly woman in a fox stole led up a dozen young lovelies. Their passage elicited from the males in the crowd a – shall we say – *dynamic* response of whistles and catcalls as the women simpered to either side, smiling, waving, throwing kisses, finally sitting themselves down with shimmying hips.

"Is that your *mother?*" I asked Doreen.

"*Hello, Mother!*" she called with a wave.

Then across the field we witnessed the arrival of Mr. and Mrs. Monopoly man, monocle and jewel-topped walking stick flashing in the sun. He looked excited, though she seemed bored.

I did regret one feature of Ohio State games: the autumn chill that permits holding hands under a blanket with one's date.

College football's pageantry began to unfold, with the added fillip of the UCLA–USC rivalry being what it was. Bands marched and tootled, cheerleaders leapt and tumbled, yell leaders led both sides' screams, to mighty feedback and mighty echoes the P.A. with lip-smacking enunciation announced players' names, and the teams ran out onto the field to roars from the crowd. All but Texas Ted. I confirmed that the Trojans' starting eleven was made up of veterans as grizzled as ours. Might be a contest!

A coin was tossed and – the Ravens' places still empty – to mounting excitement a football kicked, caught and run back. Still no sign of Ted, or of Uncle Jim, either.

Finally, the Raven brothers pushed grimly in right in front of us. Across the field Cassidy waved with both hands, which they bridled at.

"Don't give him the satisfaction," I heard Mr. Delbert tell his brother.

Spearing his top hat with his walking stick, Cassidy lofted it and waved it from side to side like a semaphore. Watching through Doreen's binoculars, I saw it fall off and get passed back to him, while Mrs. Cassidy puckered her lips at *me*. Startled, I lowered my glasses at the same instant Mr. Delbert lowered his. Looking pleased with himself, Cassidy plopped his hat back on his head.

A few hours earlier when I left them, the Ravens looked vindicated and determined. Now they seemed – deflated. What happened? Meanwhile their entourage of university officials, including Chancellor Moore, sternly took their seats.

Turning, Mr. Thomas waved me over. Dipping my head between his and his brother's, I heard Dean Miller telling them, "Week's suspension to start. Going to Texas tonight, I'll figure out this mess."

"Didn't you hear what the Sheriff said?" Mr. Delbert appealed. "'Ought to know my own son, shouldn't I? And this is Ted Groves.' That's what he *said*, Dean. Calling the Sheriff a *liar*?"

Mr. Thomas spoke tersely into my ear. "Get to the locker room and take Ted and Jim home. We'll take care of Doreen. *Damn* that Cassidy!"

"*Damn* him!" said his brother.

Doreen offering no demur, I made my way through the tunnels to UCLA's locker room.

There I found a tragic tableau, a veritable *Pietá*: Ted on a trainer's table laid out flat like a corpse, face white as marble, Jim hunched over him. Above us, cheers rocked the Coliseum as USC began racking up its score.

Clearly the worst had happened. Sick to my stomach, I asked no one in particular, "What's going on?"

"Just get us home, please, Doc," Jim said. Slowly coming to life, Ted sat up on the edge of the table, hopped off, started stripping off his uniform and pads, pulled on chinos and sports shirt and, the stadium over us resounding, we trudged out.

Not much was said on the trip to Holmby Hills.

"Get through this," I heard Jim say at one point.

"Oh, I know that, Dad. And knew it had to happen, sooner or later."

"Well," Jim said to that.

His man waved us through the gate. Crows were cawing lustily as we went up the drive; they made me shiver.

At Jim's when I returned from washing my hands, I found Ted — *Shorty* — on the living room couch holding the telephone to his ear and Jim starting up the hallway. I wasn't sure if I should just go home or what.

"We'll get going in a minute, Doc," Jim called. He'd already pulled on his tallest pair of hand-tooled, silver-embossed cowboy boots, so verged on six-and-a-half-feet high. "Waiting on long distance."

Meanwhile KEJK's announcer could barely keep up with UCLA's serial disasters on the field.

"Ted —" I asked. "*Shorty*, how you doing?"

"Oh, I'm OK, Bing," he said, adding wryly, "and you can call me Ted till they tell me that's not who I am any more."

"Would coming clean be the best idea?"

"Be the end of everything, so maybe I'll stick to my story for now." But he managed to look amused.

The radio told us, "Ten minutes to go in the second quarter, it's 18-6, USC. The loss of Texas Ted is hurting the Bruins *bad.*"

Jim came down the hall stuffing a Colt .45 revolver in his waistband—the same fine gun I'd shot Frank Holloway with those many years ago. Rummaging in a hall drawer, he pulled out a six-pointed tin star and pinned it to his breast.

"Beverly Hills," he told me. "Honorary."

Just then, the call coming through, Shorty handed him the phone and, sitting down, Jim raised his voice.

"Red, it's Jim Groves... Yeah, really is... Oh, doing fine, thanks, how are you and Arlene...? Uh-huh...? Uh-huh...?" Jim rolled his eyes at me. *"Huh!*

"Listen, Red, funny question: Anyone been sniffing around about my boys...? *Exactly...!* Well, they tell me the Dean of Men had a phone call, just wondering if it came from Vernon...? On the train headed there as we speak, sure he'll be seeing you. So if you hear anyone talking about Shorty—I mean *Ted*—please let me know... 'Shorty' just slipped out, haven't seen *Shorty* in a dog's age, someone said he's roughnecking in Louisiana, but who knows? Anyway, it's Ted out here with me... *Which* Ted? Red, line's gone all staticky, have to let you go. Bye-bye!"

Jim hung up in some haste.

"Shorty's old coach at Vernon High," he told me with the ghost of a smile, clapping his Stetson on his head. "Let's go chase this thing down. You drive."

"Think I'll go for a swim," Shorty announced.

"You do that," Jim told him.

In my car going down the drive, he told me, "What it is, seems some woman called up Dean Miller, told him *Ted's* really

Shorty. Miller won't say who. Ten minutes before the game he and Chancellor Moore *bench* him."

His man opened the gate for us and closed it smartly on the first of the reporters who would besiege the place for days.

"A *woman?*"

"That's what Miller says. But that don't mean nothing, got to be Cassidy behind it."

"Think so?"

"Who else could it be, Doc? *'Course* it's Cassidy."

"But he's got his own ringers," I said. "Why would he rat out the Ravens when they can rat *him* out right back?"

"Don't forget that bet of theirs. Fact he made it tells me he had an ace up his sleeve."

"Lot of trouble to go to for a ten-buck bet," I sniffed.

"Ten shares of Caldego Oil, $1 par value per share?" Jim asked, his hand directing me off Sunset. "Doc, that's no $10 bet: That's for control of Caldego Canyon. Ten shares tips it from equal partners to majority control. Cassidy wins, doubt the Ravens see another dime.

"*Cui bono*, isn't that what the lawyers ask? And who *bonos* here? *Cassidy!*"

"Maybe," I said skeptically. But he had a point.

"Well, we're going to treat it like a case of cattle rustling back home," he told me. "Somebody in this town knows all about it, and we just have to meet up with whoever that is, and do it before 8:00 o'clock tonight."

"Why 8:00 o'clock tonight?"

"That's when the Ravens bring their stock certificate to Cassidy's boardroom at Pan-Hemispheric."

"*If* UCLA loses."

Jim didn't bother answering.

18.

DRIVING UNCLE JIM reminded me of visiting him in Vernon when I was 12 years old and we were called out south of town to gape at the empty grave from which his father's bones had been pulled after 32 years in the ground, never to be seen again. Put-putting back to town in his official Sheriff's Model T, Jim worked through the competing interests different people might have had in those bones and solved the crime before we hit Vernon's outskirts.

Today, in *my* Ford in Beverly Hills, California, I sensed him weighing possibilities and working out permutations. If not so coolly as of yore: He seemed furious.

"What gets me is making Shorty the scapegoat," he said. "Think he's the only one stretching out his playing days? Not by a long shot."

Beverly Hills, already a famous enclave for the wealthy, was surprisingly new; the oldest movie-star homes not two decades old. But before it hosted the stars, it was a farm town — beans and oranges — so behind Burton Way there was still a strip of rickety barns and warehouses like you'd find across the tracks anywhere in Texas. A revelation to me that Beverly Hills had a seedy side.

"Never been *here*," I remarked.

The wooden building Jim had me double-park in front of

looked almost derelict, though cars lined the street. *General Store* was painted in peeling gold on a window backed by taped-up newspapers. A sign running the length of the roof read *Morocco Junction Feed.*

A man fresh from a gangster flick—dark shirt, jacket and fedora—glared at us from the cracked sidewalk in front.

He appeared to recognize my uncle.

"Well, well, if it ain't the Mayor of Beverly Hills," he said. Spitting, he gave a short nod to a similar type across the street.

"Howie," said Jim, stepping around him and going indoors. I followed. Glancing at the taped-up newspapers, I saw an old ad for a 1933 Oldsmobile: *General Motors Offers You Its Latest Achievement.*

The room—tinted sepia from the newspapers—had chalkboards ranged along the far end, rows of chairs, a radio tuned to the game and telephones constantly ringing. Men sat eyeing the chalked figures that telephone clerks were wiping off and replacing. We'd barged in on some kind of well-oiled operation. Whenever the radio announced another USC first down, men grinned or groaned.

Seeing Jim, a man with greased hair came over calling, "Mayor."

"Hey, Gino, how goes it? My nephew."

"Charmed," said Gino. "What can I do for you?"

"Any action today on the game over at the Coliseum?"

"Oh, was there?" Gino answered pleasantly. "But you mean unusual? Big wad on UCLA. Don't ask who from, because I won't tell you, but you don't need to ask, anyway."

I imagine he meant the Ravens.

"Their fullback got pulled just before the game. See it in the odds?"

"You mean the ringer?" asked Gino. "There goes the game *and* season. But you can't make money off an open secret. No, odds never budged."

"Any idea who blew the open secret open?"

"Honestly don't know. Hard lines on Texas Ted. Helluva player. Got the old paprika, that one."

"That he has," sighed Jim.

"Might go see the sign man."

"Our next stop," Jim said, turning around.

"Mayor."

Outdoors Jim advised Howie not to take any wooden nickels and directed me east on Santa Monica.

"Well, Doc," he said as we rolled along, "if the odds didn't change before the game, maybe this really did come out of left field. Which is good news. Hate to see gamblers take over college ball."

"Who put money on UCLA?"

"Who do you think?"

"There a possibility of reinstating Shorty, Jim?"

"Sure there is. He's 'suspended.' Nothing final about 'suspended.' Have to stick to our guns, find out who spilled the beans. Depending, reinstatement's a distinct possibility. But today's game was the big one."

As we drove I thought I could hear earth-shattering cheers from the Coliseum, though really it was too far away.

"Poor Shorty," Jim said. "Can say it's his own fault, but it's a shame for everybody."

"Can't he turn pro?"

"'Pro'?" he scoffed. "So broke up already, wears a tin corset some days. What he wants is to coach. Out the window without a degree. Up Vine Street, please."

At Hollywood Boulevard Jim turned us right, and at the Pantages Theater left again. Soon we were winding under Beachwood Canyon's welcoming arch and glimpsing the HOLLYWOODLAND sign rising up so immense you could almost touch it—even if, I mused, you couldn't necessarily read it any better than from the beach at Venice.

But before reaching the horse farm at the top, Jim had me turn off on a gated ridgeline driveway to a promontory where stood a majestic façade. The mansion undid its own dignity when, at the curve, we could see it was only one room thick.

As we entered a forecourt filled with sleek cars—a black Lincoln, a Cadillac convertible in yellow, a tricked-out red DeSoto—Jim had me pause as if he expected to be accosted. But there was nobody about.

"Well, go ahead and park," he said. "But let's give it a minute."

We gave it two. Someone came out then, someone who looked like he thought he was in Chicago or New York—fedora and loud double-breasted suit, though his dark glasses were pure Hollywood. After scrutinizing us, he gestured and, footsteps snapping, went to the front door.

As he got out Jim murmured, "Stay here, Doc."

I kept to his shoulder.

"Doc—" he said with exasperation, and called to the man, "He in?"

A wag of chin and brim. I followed Jim into an entry hall whose far wall was stained glass. Our guide indicated a room to the side and we went in.

"Have a seat," we were told, so sat down beside the hearth.

"Whose house is this, Uncle Jim?"

"Don't really want to know," he told me, reaching to his tin star for reassurance.

"Star looks good on you, Sheriff," called a man I hadn't known was there, standing at a far doorway. "What can I do you for?"

"UCLA—" said Jim.

"Ahh," the man said. "Big surprise, that."

"Surprise?"

"Could have knocked me down with a feather," the man said. "Really. 30-12, too!"

"That the score?"

"Just now."

Jim came to his feet.

"OK, all I wanted to know."

"Mind you, doubt Texas Ted was fooling anybody really, Sheriff, but that's baked into the product, if you know what I mean — *baked* in. Helluva football player."

"Thanks," said Jim, and led me back through that room glorious with glass and out into the open air.

We drove downhill. Though the afternoon still had the free, expansive feeling of any Saturday, darkness wasn't that far off, sunset coming at 5 o'clock; no daylight saving in that era.

"Who was that, Jim?"

"Someone who knows what he's talking about. That room we visited earlier? His, along with others up and down the coast. Takes us back to Cassidy."

He was chewing on his mustache, so I knew his best brains were at work.

"But Uncle Jim, the Trojans looked even older than the Bruins — team's *stuffed* with ringers. Don't see Cassidy taking the risk of calling out Shorty — "

"Brazen's his middle name," Jim declared.

Above us rose slopes of pink and purple. Below we could see the whole low-slung town, white and beige poking up through greenery.

"Los Angeles is the only place I know where the underworld's in plain sight," Jim said. "Coming up here, we're looking at what we want to know, if only we knew how to see it. A whole seamy underside exposed to view. And you know who's part of it?"

He fell silent, so I had to oblige.

"Who, Uncle Jim? That man up there?"

"*I* am, Doc," he said, slapping at the dashboard. "*I* am. Dammit, should have stayed in Texas. In Texas I'm an honest man. So damn mad at myself."

Nothing I could say to that.

A coyote loped high-shouldered across the road, giving us a hungry look. Fortunately we were too big for him to eat.

"Where to, Uncle Jim?"

"Police Headquarters, please, Doc."

19.

IT WASN'T FAR. We wound Downtown on Sunset, found Los Angeles Street and parked near LAPD's overstuffed Victorian bastion.

Making sure his star was still there and his hat on his head, but leaving the six-shooter under the seat, Jim led me inside and upstairs as though he knew where he was going.

On a landing a pair of policemen were bracing two young men.

"Pretty low, you ask me," one complained, "climbing fire escapes to peek through windows."

"Should keep it in your pants, faggots," a cop said with a thump of his baton.

Jim found a door that said VICE and, opening it, drawled into the room in his best Texan, "Aft'noon, y'all."

I'd noticed his accent wasn't as strong as it used to be, but now it rang out as though he were walking into his own jailhouse in Vernon, Texas. Scanning the half-staffed Saturday office, I saw faces looking around with amusement at the cowboy-hatted interloper. But one battered specimen with arrestingly innocent eyes stood up and called over, "Jim Groves."

"Hey, Clem, how's it going? My nephew Doc."

"Doc. What's on your mind, Sheriff? Come on in here, why

don't you both?"

Clem took us into a room off the larger one. It might have been used for interrogations. He flipped on a light hanging low over an old table carved with initials, names and defiant slogans, and we sat down on straight-backed chairs. It reminded me of movie detectives working over the suspect.

"It's about this game today out at the Coliseum."

Clem looked interested.

"Isn't that something?" he offered encouragingly. "Quite a turn of events."

"You know I work for Mr. Thomas Raven?"

"Sure, Jim, of course."

"And that Texas Ted Groves is my son?"

Clem leaned back, wrapping his arms around himself, surprised, if more interested than ever.

"Well, now, that's news to me. Texas Ted *your* boy? *Shit.*"

"Shit's the word."

"Is it true, Jim? He a ringer?"

"Well, maybe I should have put my foot down, though older I get, I'm impressed by how little influence – let alone *power* – a man has over his own grown sons."

Clem grunted sympathetically in that searching cone of light.

"Helluva player."

"Yep. Just wondering what Vice might know about it? If any touts or bookies – *anyone* – gave a clue he was going to be – unmasked?"

"You know I can't –" Clem started. He changed his mind. "Hell, Jim, not a peep. Surprise all around. Usually these big games – 'specially going for the Rose Bowl, conference championship, whole ball of wax? – they leave a trail: Look at the winners, who cashes in, how the odds changed and – Well, you know us, our first thought. But nothing. Bolt from the blue.

"Why? Got something for us?"

"Been down to Morocco Junction and up to the sign man's: Nothing, either place. No action, no rumors."

Clem nodded.

"What's my boy going to do now?"

"If he's got himself in a pickle, I'm sorry for it."

"What I'm bound and determined to do is find out who blabbed," said Jim. "Who ratted him out?"

"But you think you know," I put in. "*Cassidy.*"

"*Andrew* Cassidy?" said Clem. "Look, if it was Cassidy— Well, just say it *was*, what do you propose doing about it? Us either? He want bragging rights to the Rose Bowl *that* bad. . ."

"More than bragging rights," I told him. "Cassidy made a bet on the game with the Raven brothers, stakes of ten shares of stock in Caldego Oil. Winner takes control of a million barrels a year."

Clem looked surprised.

"That so, Jim? OK, good to know. Thanks. But you're not fool enough to take on *Cassidy*, are you? Men have been trying that since my grandfather's day. And you know where you'll find every single one of them? Underground.

"To say something you'll have figured out long since: When millionaires fall out? Dangerous neighborhood. You're with the Ravens, Jim? Keep your eyes open and be careful. I hear anything, let you know."

"Thanks, Clem."

Standing up into shadow, we reached under the light to shake hands.

"Good luck, Sheriff. Doc."

Night was falling when we got outside, where cops were bouncing a handcuffed Mexican off the sidewalk. Night happens in a hurry in Los Angeles, darkness dumped over the city all at once. I don't know why what I got used to in Ohio—daylight's gradual attenuation, ebbing ever so gently—happens so abruptly there, but it feels appropriate, too. That city loves its darkness.

Looking up at Bunker Hill, I saw the beacon atop the Pan-Hemispheric Petroleum Company headquarters already revolving, its brilliant shaft angling out from the center of the city and coming relentlessly around, flashing when it hit your eyes and swerving onwards to vanish before coming around again.

"Where to, Uncle Jim, West Adams?"

"Don't be cute," he said, stuffing his gun back in his waistband. "Really want to witness more joy than could do us any good? Students dancing around bonfires? No, time enough to see Cassidy at 8:00 o'clock. Let's find a drugstore, check in with Shorty."

We found a Rexall, but when he came out Jim had nothing to report.

"How's ol' Shorty holding up?"

"Fine," he said. "Head over here on Skid Row, please."

My eyes widened, but I did it, my first-ever visit.

Jim had me wind along its length, past forms recumbent on sidewalks, or sitting and drinking or fighting—vignettes of despair. New York may have its classic Bowery, where drunks—said to be mostly college professors on the skids—guzzle Thunderbird wine in doorways, but Los Angeles' own Skid Row has to be an up-and-comer. Only blocks from Broadway, it was a sad sight, and the stench memorable.

Parking, we walked up the sidewalk past barrel fires, Jim peering into every face, and came to a lot with wood-and-canvas shelters amidst bonfires—a real Hooverville.

Here he found the man he was looking for. No introductions offered as he squatted beside a bum in a watch cap who, sipping from a tin cup, large eyes reflecting flames, evinced a primordial indisposition to move. Jim plucked a bill from his wallet, folded it, laid it next to him and murmured questions.

All I could hear was, "No... No... *Nope,*" even as at one point the man gestured towards Pan-Hemispheric's rooftop light. "Keep my ears open, Sheriff, but haven't heard anything like *that.*"

"Thanks," said Jim, and we turned to go back to the car, our way mocked by red-neon script high over Broadway: *THE MILLION DOLLAR HOTEL.* Looking back, I saw our man unfold Jim's bill, iron it flat with his hand, fold it up again and put it away.

Back in the car, I said, "You sure do know a lot of people, Uncle Jim."

It sounded like something my 12-year-old self might have said. He smiled.

"Nature of the law game, Doc. Know at one time I thought you might follow in my footsteps?"

"Really?" But I remembered his patiently letting me tag along when he chased the Oklahoma Yeggman—the newsreel of it made Jim famous for a week—and when he was looking for my grandfather's snatched bones. "Think I'm better at chemistry."

"For the best, I'm sure," he said, directing me to drive west. "Well, if money was riding on this thing, no one knows about it who should. And if it's not gamblers, got to be *Cassidy.*"

He looked grim.

20.

DRIVING OUT ALONG SUNSET again, we curved through Silver Lake beneath the hilltop villas of the earliest silent-movie stars and through Sunset Junction.

At Western, Jim had me turn right. This was Doreen's neighborhood.

"Doc, might want to stay in the car, this next stop."

"Dangerous?"

He chuckled.

"Only to a gentleman's sensibilities. One of Hollywood's more select houses. Lord knows, no shortage of brothels in this town, but these ladies usually know what's going on. Be glad: If Prohibition were still on, we'd be chasing bootleggers, too.

"Pull up over here."

And he directed me to the curb in front of a big house with a turret — Doreen's house.

"Be right back," Jim said.

"Coming with you."

I followed him up the walk. As we approached the porch, lights came on, the door swung open and Mrs. Vorhees called, "Evening, Sheriff, that day of the week already? But glad to see you. Your friends bought out the house, then had to go and *lose*. Loneliest party you ever did see." Her voice was — how to put it? — *suggestive,* until, seeing me, she got flustered. "Why, *Bing!*"

Passing into the stair hall, Jim took off his hat. Through open doors, I could see boarders sitting around the parlor.

I suppose *boarders* is a misnomer.

"Here on business, Mrs. Vorhees."

"Always, Sheriff."

"Hear any talk about my boy getting pulled from the game?"

"Keep telling you to bring him by, he'd find his biggest rooters right under my roof. Sorry about what happened today— Hell, we were there, *right, girls?* Keep our ears open, but it was a surprise to us."

Jim thanked her, was shifting his weight preparatory to turning around, replacing his Stetson and leaving, when Doreen started down the stairs.

"*Bing!*" she said brightly, but seeing Jim, her mother and the women in the next room, she stepped slower and slower and at the bottom gripped the banister with knuckles white as her face.

If she didn't know what to say, neither did I. Nodding at her, I walked out of the house, Jim followed and I drove away from there like an automaton.

So Doreen's mother was a whore. Not Doreen; her *mother*. Well, in the history of the Republic, millions of mothers have been whores, whether anyone chooses to remember the fact or not (and they prefer not to, thanks very much). I even wondered whether Doreen's prospector-father wasn't a figment of someone's imagination.

So what of Doreen?

Not the girl for me, I decided; or not decided, but *knew*, no thought required. Not her fault, and so very conventional of me. But it just wouldn't work.

In silence we drove down Hollywood Boulevard's Saturday-night gaudiness for a while before Jim said, "Sorry about that, Doc."

"Not your fault, Jim."

"Do wish life was different from the way it is," he said. "Nothing I can do about it, though, that's for sure.

"The nub of life—*point* of it—for most people comes down to *money*, but what a body does for money can pollute the kind of. . . of *purity* it takes to negotiate life with any self-respect, not to mention *autonomy*. There, I'm using bigger words than you thought I knew. But I'm trying to say something, Doc."

"I know it, Jim."

"Every tough guy I ever met holds dear and certain that life's a fight against his fellow man. Something kicked into him by the age of seven that, long as he lives, remains life's big fact.

"And life's sure enough *hard,* but to see it as a fight like that? Have to be better than that or we're just animals. Look at the Depression, Doc: People starving right here in America, but everybody's at each other's throats anyway, trying to get ahead every moment, trample their fellow man if that's what it takes. Just business—*everything's* just business.

"I think back to Texas— Remember seeing thunderheads rearing themselves up, miles high and heaven-bright? Scary as it is to hear God rearranging His furniture up there?"

"Sure do, Uncle Jim."

"That's how big this world is, but people prefer to reduce it to a ledgerbook page. Feel *safer* that way. Our Ravens have some good ideas— I mean, they're right, Los Angeles is going to grow, and they're going to get even richer than they are now, but. . ."

He lapsed into silence, before quietly saying, "On the hunt there for something that seems to have eluded me, Doc. But there's more to life than most people imagine."

After another silence he said, "Thing I keep coming back to is Shorty playing football—packing the ball, making interference, feinting left, feinting right, running through the lines. *Kicking.* Boy's made to play that game. Makes it a thing of beauty, and *beauty* hasn't got a price tag."

204

"Except at Mrs. Vorhees' house."

Jim sighed. "Except at Mrs. Vorhees' house. Hungry, Doc?"

"Starving."

"Let's find some chow before we meet up with Cassidy and the Ravens. Musso's OK?"

21.

SOON WE WERE SEATED in a booth sipping martinis and eating chicken à-la-king.

"Covered some ground today, Doc. One thing about California, get in your car, soon enough you're someplace else. Not like Texas. Driving anywhere in Texas generally leaves you someplace just like where you started."

Every few minutes fellow diners greeted Jim—shot their arms over the table to shake his hand. "Sheriff," they'd say, and to me, "Must be proud of your uncle."

"Going in tonight to sign over control of a million-dollar operation," Jim said. "Should be no problems, 'less Cassidy starts to gloat, and then I can't answer for Mr. Thomas or his brother, or for me. But he won't gloat. No need to."

"He'll gloat," I said. "You kidding?"

Jim swallowed before saying, "Well, just better not. Ravens are in no mood. Losing this bet—and those monthly cheques—could put the kibosh to their business."

"I remember the day they made that bet," I said. "Seemed so innocent."

"Cassidy's innocent as a rattlesnake. Should be legal to shoot him on sight, but any problems, it's *your* fault doing business with a rattlesnake in the first place."

He pushed his plate away.

206

"Boy, did that hit the spot. Doc, might be best if you went home right now."

"Coming with you, Uncle Jim."

"One phone call, then, and we'll *git*," he said. Untucking his napkin, he got up and went to the bar. Stuffing a napkin in his shirt was one of Uncle Jim's embarrassing hick habits, but I'd begun to suspect that, to an extent anyway, he was putting it on.

The bartender tilted his head to Jim's, placed a telephone on the bar's copper top, Jim picked it up and turned away.

A minute later, his shoulders were collapsing and he was caving in on himself. When he tottered back and slipped into the banquette he was glassy-eyed.

"Well, how you like them apples?" he rumbled. "Shorty just had a Western Union from his brother Ted back home: Guess who it was called the Dean of Men on him? His old high-school English teacher, Mrs. Pemmican."

"Not *Cassidy?*"

"Nope. You were right, Doc, guess Cassidy wasn't going to upset his own apple cart."

But I was staggered. I'd long since changed my mind: *Had* to be Cassidy.

"She saw his picture in the Vernon *Record* after the Stanford game, and was bothered to see *Shorty* Groves identified as someone called *Texas Ted* Groves. Took it on herself to set them straight. Shit, can't make this stuff up.

"Tell you, my mind's been churning: If not Cassidy, was it maybe Mr. Delbert's *woman?* Headed for some kind of drama, *that* pair.

"Lordy, what a turn. Don't talk to me about price tags! Shorty cheated, and I didn't stop him. Hell, why would I, when I got a job and a cottage out of the deal? Corrupt as I am, I walked right into it. But *they* set the trap!

"The scales have dropped from my eyes, Doc: It's *them!* It's us against *them,* always has been, always will be, forever and ever, amen. But they have us right where they want us.

"*Shit.* Where's our waiter? I need another drink. Then it's on to our appointment in Damascus."

I needed another one myself.

"Hurts my son worst of all. His name's tainted forevermore."

"Well, not *his* name," I murmured.

Funny thing: As we were leaving, Stan Laurel walked in right past us, but we didn't recognize him — not until Tuesday, when Louella Parsons' *Examiner* column said: "Oliver Hardy's favorite partner dined at Musso & Frank's Saturday night!"

22.

WE HURRIED DOWNTOWN, Uncle Jim pointing out as we passed it the compact pumpjack still laboring atop Cassidy's very first, hand-dug well in Echo Park.

Ahead of us on Bunker Hill rose the Pan-Hemispheric Petroleum building, Downtown's highest point, its revolving arc light shooting a lighthouse-bright ray that made the Public Library's mosaic ziggurat stand out against the Biltmore Hotel's brick. What struck me was how the light seemed to palm the mosaic, get slowed up a little before it swept around again seconds later.

We had to park two blocks away and walk over to where Mr. Delbert's Cadillac V-16 sat idling beneath the Biltmore; no chauffeur tonight. The Ravens had set the rendezvous perhaps not realizing that merriment from USC's victory party in the ballroom overhead would wash over them while they waited for us.

We got in the backseat. That interior was rank with rage.

"Well, Sheriff?" said Mr. Delbert. "Get proof the old thief squealed on your son?"

"*Wa-al* now," said Jim, reverting to his best hayseed manner, "guess I know what you want me to say, and I'm sincerely sorry *and* more than a tad surprised that I cannot say it."

"*Fuck,*" said Mr. Thomas. "*Had* to be Cassidy."

Mr. Delbert said, "Got Shorty benched to win this fucking bet!"

"We're pretty steamed, Sheriff."

"*Wa-al,* I gather that. Can only tell you what I found. Went into it deep since the game, gentlemen, and Cassidy had nothing to do with it. Didn't bet on it, or if he had a flutter, nothing compared to what you two put on it.

"No, fact is, it was my son's old schoolteacher back in Texas who telephoned Dean Miller. After the Stanford game Mrs. Pemmican saw Shorty's picture in the paper captioned 'Texas Ted Groves.' Thought she was correcting a typographical error."

"*Teacher?*" erupted Mr. Delbert, his brother shouting, "Damn *teacher?*"

They looked at each other, but if they communicated anything, I wasn't privy to it. Mr. Thomas adjusted the mirror so he could drill Jim through it.

"Why, Sheriff, this just knocks everything out from under you and your son."

"Yep."

"Unless —" said Mr. Delbert. "Unless you come upstairs with us, Jim, be a part of it."

"Going upstairs, but won't be part of anything, tell you now. Suggest you gentlemen give *me* the stock certificate, and I'll get your bet paid off without any trouble."

"Not the plan," said one of them.

"Bing, you stay here," my uncle told me.

"I'm coming," I said.

Mr. Delbert turned around and said, "Bing, upstairs if anyone happens to go out on the terrace for a smoke or something, stay in your seat. Cassidy always wants to show off the view, but whatever happens, you stay indoors. Clear?"

"Yes, sir," I said, and we hushed, for who should choose this fraught moment to amble out of the Biltmore and cross the sidewalk to the Packard limousine waiting in front of us? Monopoly man himself, on his arm Mrs. Monopoly in a slinky gown sparkling with sequins and a white fur stole even brighter than her hair, serious diamonds cinching her throat.

Amidst thunder, the motorcycle escort's engines started up and the cavalcade went into motion, going around the block before pulling up exactly one block behind us at Pan-Hemispheric Petroleum. Turning around, I saw Cassidy toddling into the building with his wife.

Mr. Delbert gunned his motor, did a punishing U-turn— going up on the sidewalk, scattering a couple walking along it— and squealed up to Pan-Hemispheric, again parking behind Cassidy's waiting procession. It was 8:00 o'clock.

To me Jim repeated, "No need for you to come upstairs."

I repeated, "I'm coming."

Looking grim, Mr. Thomas got out and, carrying a portfolio, so did his brother. Jim didn't hesitate, so I got out, too. Putting back my head to take in the building's 12 handsome stories, I saw the light shooting around and around.

We crossed the sidewalk. It was up to me, as the junior, to pull at a door: *Locked*. A doorman inside promptly stepped forward and pushed it open, with nothing said.

The lofty lobby—bearing a hint of jasmine—had marble floors, a gilt coffered ceiling and bronze electroliers. Murals depicted California's wealth and history—Forty-Niners, fleets of ships, locomotives, fields of produce, orchards, forests, tribes kneeling to priests, Cassidy Memorial Library. In place of honor was a mural featuring Cassidy as a young man, a spade in his hands and gladness lighting up his dark-mustached face while a protective umbrella of black gold spouted behind.

An attendant in an elevator scented with jasmine took us up to the penthouse floor. No one said a word.

The attendant cranked open the doors to a lobby like the one downstairs: marble floor, golden ceiling, alabaster standing lamps, a trace of jasmine.

The brothers knew their way around. They led us through a waiting area, past porphyry obelisks flanking the open door of an opulent office where Mrs. Cassidy sat peering into her handbag, to the double doors of the boardroom of the Pan-Hemispheric Petroleum Company. Two large men posted there stepped forward, and we stood like dogs getting toweled off after a bath while they frisked us.

One found Uncle Jim's Colt and sardonically held it up.

"Don't let me forget that on the way out," Jim told him.

Entering that boardroom, it was palpable that we were in the seat of power in California.

More than the State Capitol or Governor's Mansion, it was from this room that power flowed throughout the State and the West. It *smelled* of it, too — an impressive, if not very pleasing, organic quintessence of bodily exhalations. A long polished table that could seat 30 dominated it, gilt-trimmed chairs sitting at it, more waiting behind. A terrace wrapped around three sides of the room, French doors piercing each silk-striped wall. The coved ceiling was painted like an arbor, tendrils plaiting crystal chandeliers. In muffled fashion we could hear the city below nervous with traffic.

Two chairs were occupied. At the far end sat Cassidy, the Oil King himself. Two places nearer sat a man I recognized, Browning, the Ravens' Caldego Canyon bookkeeper.

Another bodyguard stood at the French doors behind Cassidy.

Mr. Delbert placed his portfolio on the near end of the table, yanked out a chair and sat down, his brother taking a seat around the corner.

"Oh, come closer than *that*, gentlemen," Cassidy piped up.

"No reason to make this more difficult than it has to be."

"We're all right here," Mr. Delbert offered.

Meanwhile Jim went half-way up the table and sat down, I next to him.

"This end, Jim?" Mr. Thomas called.

"This is fine," Jim answered. "Switzerland."

Cassidy barked a laugh.

The light in that room was extraordinary. Radiating from the chandeliers, it bounced between ceiling and glossy tabletop to produce a glow whose intensity seemed keyed to the general tension. Sitting down, through the uncurtained doors opposite me I could see the parapet pulsing with the beacon's light and, beyond, blank mountains against moonless sky.

Cassidy leaned back and gestured. "Ever see such a beautiful room? Built it in the year '29—high-water mark for us all, I daresay," he said. "My library at home's nice, but *this* gives me my city, my state: Can see it all from up here. That beacon up top? My idea. Oh, should see the Edison bill! But 50 miles out at sea they see *Cassidy's* light, know this is *Cassidy's* town!"

He got down to business.

"Well, gentlemen, glad there's no welshing with the Raven brothers. Not the way I wanted to win our bet, but if your team's best player was a *ringer...!*" He shook his head mockingly. "Please give Mr. Browning your certificate for ten shares in the Caldego Oil Company."

No one moved.

Amused, Cassidy said, "Mr. Browning, I'm afraid you're going to have to go get it. Believe you're acquainted? Oh, Mr. Browning and I go way back."

And he chortled as Browning went down the table, the Raven brothers flushing as they registered the fact that their man at Caldego Canyon was in reality Cassidy's man, that their bad day had just gotten worse.

"Mr. Browning will cross out your names, write mine in, we'll sign and countersign, he'll make the corresponding entries in his ledger and we'll all have some champagne. If you want we can even shake hands—up to you. On Monday, Pan-Hemispheric's Registrar will inform our transfer agent at Wells Fargo."

Mr. Delbert stared long and hard at Cassidy while Browning, waiting embarrassed at his elbow, blushed.

Mr. Thomas finally reached into his brother's portfolio, took out a stiff, green-engraved document and handed it to Browning, while saying down the table, "As it happens, Mr. Cassidy, my brother and myself wish to discuss Caldego Canyon: We know what you're up to out there—moving as much crude by night as by day."

"Oh dear, oh dear, what's this you say?" Cassidy said humorously.

Mr. Delbert growled, "We took you into partnership for your expertise—not for you to bilk us."

Back at his seat, Browning dabbed at the inkwell in front of him and with a scratchy sound inscribed the certificate, then opened a leather-bound volume gilt-stamped *Pan-Hemispheric Petroleum Co.*

"On Monday," said Mr. Thomas, "our attorneys will inform the California Oil and Gas Commission—*and* the Internal Revenue Service—that you've been bilking *them,* too, and moreover they will file suit against Pan-Hemispheric and you personally for past-due payments to us, as well as triple damages."

His brother took it up. "You better believe we're going to get your books and take a magnifying glass to them."

Browning handing him the certificate, Cassidy peered through his monocle, signed his name and leaned back with a yellow smile.

"Do as you must," he remarked. "I'll take my chances in the courts, as I always have. Makes no difference to what we're here to do tonight. Mr. Browning, please have my partners affix their signatures, and then you may open the champagne."

The Ravens with no good grace signing their names, Browning placed the certificate on top of his ledger and at the sideboard began untwisting the wires of an iced bottle: *Pop!* He poured six flutes and carried them around clinking and jittering on a tray.

"Gentlemen, may I propose a toast?" Cassidy said, pushing himself to his feet and raising his glass. *"To the Trojans!"*

"The *hell* —!"

"Never – !"

"So sensitive," said Cassidy, smirking. "Then how's this: *To a great rivalry!* That do, *hmm?*"

It sufficed, and we drank (not really champagne; sparkling wine from his vineyard up north).

"Now then, come see my view!" he said. "Don't get up *here* every day. You, too, Sheriff, Bing: Never seen anything like it!"

The bodyguard opening the doors, Cassidy carried his glass out to the terrace and the Ravens got up and followed. Jim stayed where he was, and his hand on my thigh arrested *me*.

At the doorway Mr. Delbert looked back and barked, "Coming, Sheriff?"

"All right here, thanks," Jim muttered.

Stiffening, Mr. Delbert went out. The bodyguard remained at the open doors. Through them to us huddled high on the bridge of the SS *California* came the wash of cool evening air and the sound of honking horns.

This was it, I knew — the moment when the Ravens might salvage half-ownership of Caldego Oil by pitching their partner over the side. Cassidy stood with a hand on the parapet and with his walking stick was pointing out something down in Pershing

Square. Its jewel flashed in the beacon's light as the Ravens moved in behind him.

Uncle Jim sighed and I held my breath. I'd never seen murder done before.

But their nerve failed, or maybe their plan depended on Jim's helping, or maybe the bodyguard's presence deterred them, or maybe they never intended murder at all, because when the brothers parted, Cassidy was still waving his stick at the horizons of his domain.

As they trailed back indoors the Ravens shot my uncle sharp glances. At Cassidy's gesture his bodyguard left the doors open.

Apparently ready to leave, the Ravens stayed on their feet, and I sensed Jim was about to get up, too. But taking his seat again, Cassidy decided to needle my uncle.

"Hell of a thing, Sheriff, that game today," he said, sipping his wine and smacking his lips. "A *ringer* at fullback? A *tramp athlete* — and your *son? Shocking.* College football's supposed to be for the *kids* — sportsmanship, fair play, school spirit, *fun.* Ringers soil what should be *pure.* You should be ashamed of yourself, Sheriff!"

"*Wa-al*, Mr. Cassidy, can't say I *am* ashamed," Jim replied. "Might have been wrong, but I only did what any true father would do."

Mr. Thomas, watching, sank back into his chair, while his brother seemed impatient to get going.

"My son shouldn't have done it, sure. Wrong to pretend to be somebody else.

"But know what's worse? You fellers trying to make money off him and his teammates in the first place — betting a million barrels of oil on their talent. Makes me sick, because you're doing it on the backs of boys who do what *they* do 'cause they don't have much choice in the matter: Shows enough hypocrisy to choke us all. It's the Depression, people!"

Jim was getting angrier by the word.

"The worst thing isn't *Shorty's* going by *Ted*, it's that people who knew exactly *who* he was—and how dirty college ball is because their money *makes* it dirty—*recruited* him." He turned to the Ravens. "Shorty was supposed to be your ticket to the Rose Bowl? Now that he's exposed, he's on his own—*he's* punished and you big boys go untouched. Bet you this, the newspapers won't mention any of *you*."

"Don't think I'll take that bet, Uncle Jim," I breathed to myself.

Through the French doors opposite me something briefly dampened the parapet's pulsing, as though someone were slipping down the terrace, but I couldn't see who, and thought nothing of it anyway. To us at the table the beacon up above carried the merest vibration as it raked city, mountains and sea.

"Cut the crap, Sheriff," said Cassidy. "Tramp athletes take chances away from deserving youngsters."

"That's right," put in Mr. Thomas, his brother adding, "You failed your son, Sheriff."

"Millionaires want you to know *they're* the ones telling the story here," Uncle Jim thundered. "It's *their* version, every time. Meanwhile, the fall guy is who he always is.

"Hypocrites, all of you: First you corrupt my son and me, then you call us corrupt! Sick and tired of it, gentlemen: It's got to *end*."

And end it did.

How, with Jim's score-settling Colt no longer on his person?

Because, as if on cue, we found ourselves in a different movie altogether.

The bodyguard—distinctly nonplussed—stepping aside for her, her head fallen back under the weight of her suffering, but embracing her martyr's fate, too, dramatic as Garbo, Mrs. Cassidy entered through the open doors, her stole wreathing her outspread arms, her trailing hand holding the sequined clutch from which she'd taken the pearl-handled automatic she held in the other.

Hiccupping a sob, she took aim (at the far end of the room, it seemed to me), closed her eyes, someone—had to be one of the Ravens—fanned off the lights, Uncle Jim pushed me under the table, and *pom! pom! pom! pom! pom! pom! pom! pom! click! click! click! click! click!*

Trying to get to my feet, I slammed my head on the table's underside, even as groans and a cloud mixed of gunpowder and jasmine filled the air. For a minute the only light was what bounced off the terrace but, the chandeliers blazing up again, I crawled out from under, as it happened near Browning, whose face rested in a puddle of blood.

What I saw was Jim in the corner propping Cassidy on his feet, the old man's shirtfront blossoming red—Jim *protecting* him while the bodyguard glazedly regarded the arm where *he'd* been shot.

Then the other bodyguards rushed in and ran up the length of the table, guns drawn, and disarmed Mrs. Cassidy.

"Oh, Daddy, wasn't aiming at you," she wailed. "Take your crummy mitts off of me!"

Jim relinquishing the Oil King, the guards settled him back into his chair, one asking, "Are you hit bad, Mr. Cassidy?"

"No, dammit, I'm not hit," Cassidy gasped indignantly, still bleeding. "Call the District Attorney!"

"How 'bout we get an ambulance first?" Uncle Jim suggested reasonably, and at the sideboard's telephone a bodyguard asked the Operator for Good Samaritan Hospital.

"No ambulance!" Cassidy managed, so instead he asked for the D.A.'s office.

Jim might have denounced them as hypocrites, but everybody I saw was behaving sincerely enough. The Raven brothers went up to Browning and set about reversing the stock transfer — blotted up the blood, scratched out the new name, wrote the old ones back in — as Cassidy tried his best to breathe and his wife wept at what had befallen her husband.

Replacing the certificate in his portfolio, Mr. Delbert and his brother turned and left the room. Mrs. Cassidy didn't appear to notice, nor did Mr. Cassidy raise an objection, except for a muttered, *"Welshers after all."*

He concentrated on his breathing, but his breaths didn't appear to take. With bodyguards huddled over him, his wife weeping into his lap, he looked like a goner for sure.

Then the men on either side stood him up and walked him out like a sack of potatoes. Cassidy managed to hold his head high, though; in Los Angeles we're all actors.

Still emoting, Mrs. Cassidy followed.

Like I said, it was from some other movie.

Retrieving his Colt from the man who'd taken it away from him — who returned it with an expression even more sardonic — Jim said, "Come on, Bing, you can drive me home."

My only thought? *He didn't call me* Doc!

When we reached the street, Cassidy's cars and motorcycles were pulling away and sirens approaching.

"Well, that was funny," Jim said as we loped along. "Biggest speech of my life, but who knows what I was going on about? Guess I wanted 'em to see what they've done to Shorty. Wouldn't cost 'em anything to admit it, either, but boy, these millionaires don't give *nothin'* away."

"Who was she aiming at?"

"Imagine Mr. Delbert. Well, I say that, but maybe Mr. Thomas? Way she shoots, lucky any of us survived."

As we got to my Ford two unmarked cars with sirens in their grilles passed.

"D.A., after all," Jim said. Which undoubtedly was why poor

Browning's obituary two days later merely noted that he'd died unexpectedly.

"What's going to happen to her, Uncle Jim?"

"Inheriting her millions a little sooner than she expected, that's all. She'll get over it.

"Murder done by millionaires? That's the kind of crime no one can solve."

23.

I DROVE UNCLE JIM home to Holmby Hills—past reporters camped at the gates waiting to catch sight of Shorty—where he insisted I take a guest room.

When I woke up late Sunday morning, he fed me breakfast on the veranda, and I accepted his invitation to stay another night: "Our house, till they boot us out."

Crows were cawing, and I told him how it made me shiver to hear them.

"*Pets*, didn't you know?" he said. "The Ravens cultivate 'em, feed 'em over at Mr. Delbert's. Very proud of 'em. Crows, ravens, Tower of London—get it? Can drive you crazy, though, I know."

Oh, OK.

They were still cawing as I reached for the *Times*. Naturally my cousin featured prominently:

UCLA FOOTBALL STAR AN IMPOSTOR
GRID HOAX PROVES "TED" IS "SHORTY"

I remember Shorty's expression that morning as being like an animal's when it realizes it's about to be slaughtered. I asked how the whole thing began.

"Fell into it real easy, Bing," he told me. "Came out here to see the '32 Olympics, and liked California right away. Picked up a quick hundred bucks playing a game against the Fleet for the

San Pedro Longshoremen under the name of a buddy back home, Joe Gelhausen. We won, too.

"Well, the Ravens were there, scouting. Introduced themselves and, what with one thing and another, put me in at Urban Military. Played there that fall, then since '33 for the Bruins.

"Knew it might come crashing down, but hoped to get my degree first. All I want is to coach."

Later, with Miss Raven, we went swimming.

"Sho-*Ted,*" she said. "Why, I had no idea! Who'd have thought it? But a Shorty by any other name. . . "

"Smells as sweet?" he offered.

"*Smells,*" she said, and dove laughing into the water, pursued by a Bruin.

But by Monday Sunday's momentous event relegated Shorty to the sports pages:

ANDREW CASSIDY, OIL KING, DIES OF LONG ILLNESS AT 78

Column after column told of Cassidy's final triumph, so surprising to everyone who knew him—*viz.,* dying in bed, of a malady not specified, holding his loving wife's hand. They outlined his career *founding* and *developing* California's *(and Mexico's)* oil industry, discovering no fewer than eight oilfields. Only glancing allusions to Teapot Dome appeared, along with a decorous paragraph about his son's death at the hands of a deranged employee.

Then came lists of his holdings and donations. We were assured that he was far the richest man in the West, his net worth—despite grievous Depression losses—estimated at $160,000,000.

Well, *that* was disappointing. Only *$160,000,000?*

I called in sick, not sure I wanted to work at Caldego Oil any longer (though what choice did I really have?). When I was getting ready to go home, Shorty said, "Favor to ask, Bing: Drop me on campus? Like to pick up a *Daily Bruin*."

"Sure thing."

We drove over through the fragrant day. Assuring me he could find his own way back, Shorty jumped out at the Janss Steps and within moments was mobbed by students who flocked up calling, "We're with you, Texas Ted!" From every quarter boys and girls came squealing up: "Ted, it's so *unfair!*"

Shortly after I got home, the phone rang. It was Aline Barnsdall. Having heard from Doreen about my "changed circumstances," she asked me to afternoon tea.

On second sight, Hollyhock House appeared to me the most beautiful I'd ever seen. Her butler showed me into the living room, where the light-drenched lawn seemed part of the furnishings, and Miss Barnsdall swept in, again in Fortuny pleats and precisely marcelled hair. Tea wasn't offered, but cocktails were.

I told her how much I liked her house.

"Thank you. Well, oil can do nice things when you're as fortunate as I am. Bing, I'm so glad Doreen brought us together. Whatever the troubles between you, I hope you can work them out. I know you will.

"Now, then, you know the Barnsdall Oil Company refinery in Oklahoma produces more wax than any plant in the world?"

"Yes?"

"Tommy Raven tells me — Doreen prompted me to ask — that you might be open to a new challenge. As it happens, Barnsdall has an opening for second assistant plant manager, and I'd be so pleased if you took the job."

Well! We talked salary, very satisfactorily, and she offered me tenancy of a sandstone Tudor on Barnsdall's Main Street that had a pumpjack sawing away in the middle of the pavement out front. It's famous — you've seen it in *Ripley's Believe It or Not!*

Of course I accepted, and agreed to get myself out there as soon as possible.

I went to bed that night in a good mood — heartened, too, by the *Daily Bruin*'s hope that "*Texas Ted* will be restored to membership on the football squad." It recounted team captain Bob McChesney's spontaneously telling a campus crowd, "That fellow who didn't play with us Saturday? He's still ace-high with us, I don't know how you feel about it."

They showed how they felt by cheering madly.

24.

ALL TOLD, THE UPROAR about Shorty played out as Jim predicted. The AP and UP pushed out story after story that every newspaper in the country printed. "Doesn't know if he's *himself,* his *brother* or his *cousin!*" was the refrain, as everyone wondered who in the world the *real* Texas Ted Groves might be (which, not that it mattered, wasn't Shorty's brother or cousin at all, but a fellow he'd roughnecked with in Mexico and whose Panhandle, Texas high-school credentials he'd borrowed, with permission).

Things came unraveled as the week wore on.

You'd think—or hope, anyway—that having delivered so noble a speech uncovering to the Ravens their own dirty motives (*and* having doubled their oil revenues), Uncle Jim would get a raise in pay and Shorty a job. But no, Mr. Thomas fired Jim and evicted them both.

It meanwhile occurred to me that perhaps, with one big swallow, I could accept Doreen's background as not being her fault. Tuesday morning, I called her up at the Dome to suggest lunch at Crawford Drugs.

She met me there, crossing the street with a brisk and businesslike step, explaining as she shook my hand that she had only half an hour, and also that my old clients, the Willards, had signed a contract that morning.

"They're building—*above* Wilshire—a $20,000 home," she

said with well-deserved satisfaction.

I was glad for her. Nervously I worked the conversation around to my new job in Oklahoma, my wish for a helpmeet, my feelings for —

She didn't let me get far.

"Bing, I'm flattered, but I'm only now getting anywhere professionally, and I need to see where it takes me. Do wish you every success. You understand, don't you?"

No, not at all, I thought as I said, "Of course."

And sadly watched her brisk return to the Dome. I think I never forgave her that impatient glance at her wristwatch as she crossed the street.

Cassidy's funeral was held two days later at St. Vincent de Paul's. It was inescapable, featured on the radio and in the papers and newsreels. Not only was the church packed, but crowds surrounded it. I believe it was George Jessel who said of the spectacle, "You see, give the people what they want and they'll come."

Cops stopping traffic at every intersection, motorcycle outriders escorted hearse and the Cassidy limousines to Calvary Cemetery. There the casket was placed in the family mausoleum beside the son's and the bronze doors closed again.

Mrs. Cassidy inherited most everything and, last I heard, is still generous to the Archdiocese, still having round-the-clock Masses said for her late husband's soul. Nor has she remarried, though rumors about her affairs vie with those about Mae West's. How long, or whether, she went on seeing Mr. Delbert, I don't know.

No funeral was held for Shorty, but really there should have been. With evidence emerging every day from former teammates and high schools and colleges about his long career as a pigskin phenom, the tide turned slowly but decisively against him. Friday was his birthday. There was no party, but

Dean Miller, back from Texas, summoned him to campus so he could deliver his findings in person. At Shorty's request, I went along for moral support.

On the way over I asked how he was doing.

"Holding up, Bing. I'm fine."

"Aren't you mad?"

"*Mad?* Naw. My own fault. And football's been good to me. No complaints."

Whether campus sentiment remained in Shorty's favor now that his guilt seemed clear I wasn't sure until we climbed the Janss Steps. Then it became obvious. No crowds ran up to be sanctified by a touch or wave. Instead, as Shorty went smiling along, big as life in his letter sweater—couldn't take *that* away from him—students stopped short at funny angles, mute and giving no signs of recognition. When we entered Kerckhoff Hall one boy hissed. That shook us up.

The Dean kept us waiting only a few minutes before admitting us to his office overlooking the quad.

It was good Shorty was prepared for the worst, because that's what he got. Dean Miller told us in detail about his lightning trip to Texas and exhaustive investigation, interviewing family, teammates, coaches and his telephonic informant, leading to his final determination that Shorty be expelled.

When he mentioned Mrs. Pemmican's telephone call, Shorty's face lighted up.

"Mrs. Orville Pemmican, my high-school English teacher," he said. "Good teacher, too—if on the strict side. Yes, I remember her in her house off the courthouse square, rocking in her chair on a hooked rug."

"Well, she remembers you, too," sniffed the Dean. "Told me she didn't want this *Texas Ted* character getting credit for *Shorty's* winning the Stanford game, and that's why she called me."

Shorty just sighed.

"Hard lines on you, Ted — I mean *Shorty*," said the Dean. "No victories will be vacated, but we're not going to the Rose Bowl this year. That's *your* fault. The lawyers tell me —"

"'First, let's kill all the lawyers,'" Shorty quoted from the Bard as he came to his feet and put out a hand. "No hard feelings, Dean."

As we walked back to my car, scattering students from our path, Shorty appeared preoccupied.

"You know Mr. Thomas sent Ruth to finishing school up north?"

"Oh, shoot," I said. "What are you going to do?"

"Well, Victor's signing me to his Lighthorse team, and seeing if he can't get me into pictures."

Victor was Victor McLaglen, the English movie star (and neighbor of the Ravens), whom Shorty had met playing rugby in the off season and who had just finished building, at Riverside and Hyperion, his remarkable 12,000-seat *Victor McLaglen Sports Center* to house his Lighthorse cavalry troop, motorcycle club and semi-pro football team.

"How about your Dad?"

"Going back to the ranch in Texas. What's left of it."

DEAN MILLER SOLEMNLY announcing Shorty's expulsion, it was open season on my cousin. The press was brutal. The *Times* applauded his being "beheaded by the faculty ax," further awarded him "a bushel of brickbats for besmirching the game of football," and proclaimed:

> Had he been at West Point, "Texas Ted" would be paraded before the cadets, the insignia cut off his uniform, his sword broken and thrown into a grave.

Bit harsh?

The next day, Shorty came clean at last. Helped by an *Examiner* sportswriter, over his own byline ("by Shorty Groves") he published his side of the story:

WANTED DEGREE, SAYS
OUSTED GRIDDER
Really Kept Nose in
Text-books, Groves Declares

It was a nice piece, forthcoming and apologetic:

> I wanted that degree, and football was helping me to get it. I got a job as caretaker of the campus tennis courts and managed to save enough money to bring my best friend— my dad, James D. Groves—to Los Angeles from Texas. It didn't matter to him whether I was *Shorty* or *Ted* as long as I was getting an education. That's what he wanted.

He and Jim followed up the column by meeting reporters in Victor McLaglen's living room, where, a hand on his son's shoulder, Jim declared, "I'm not ashamed of what he did, or what I did, either. Any true father would have done the same."

Shorty admitted that he was wrong to have played after his eligibility expired, apologized for pretending to be someone he wasn't, said he was sorry and implored forgiveness from his teammates, Coach Spaulding and the whole UCLA community.

"I've learned my lesson. Swear to God I only did it because I wanted a college education. Finally realized a fellow can't get any place in this world without it, but I didn't have money for college unless I played football."

It seemed to go over, the earnest young *(youngish)* scholar and his fond papa, and some of the resulting stories were sympathetic. But, as one reporter put it, it was too late to "unring the ringer." In the end Shorty's confession did him no good. That he'd stuck to his story until he couldn't any longer made some people feel doubly deceived.

I always thought sticking to his story just a rookie error.

Curiously—or maybe not—as Jim predicted, in the whole brouhaha about Shorty, the nationwide sensation called the *Great Groves Mystery* or the *Hidden Identity Play,* the Raven name never appeared, except TIME magazine mentioned Shorty's former residence on Mr. Thomas's estate.

Of course, there was no real mystery about Shorty's identity—not to him, anyway. Playing football for a dozen years under four names at three high schools and three colleges, Shorty Groves knew exactly who he was—someone gifted with an extraordinary talent he loved sharing with the world.

When I showed up at work to clear out my desk—retrieve my glass paperweight—I found the building in an uproar.

The Ravens' lawyers, working with Cassidy's, were installing new managers who announced that no changes would be made. But everything was different already. A Raven lawyer took notice of me and demanded the car Mr. Thomas gave me the money to buy. Got home that day via Red Car.

We arranged our respective moves quickly. Moving into a cottage behind Victor McLaglen's mansion, Shorty took charge of the star's tennis court. Jim kindly offered to drop me off at Barnsdall, Oklahoma on his way to Bugscuffle, Texas. *Elliott.* I was grateful.

Dad and Violet saw us off early on Sunday, I riding shotgun in Uncle Jim's milkman's pickup, the bed piled high with our things. This time we really did look like Okies. The sun was washing the streets clean as we wended through Downtown on Route 66, Pan-Hemispheric's beacon extinguished.

Uncle Jim remarked ruefully, "Don't think I'll miss California much, Bing, 'cept maybe for the climate. Nice playground for millionaires, but you have to like the way millionaires play—which is for *keeps.*"

It was a good trip.

YEARS LATER, in L.A. on business, I took a few hours to drive out to Caldego Canyon, and even had lunch at the clubhouse. By golly, a dozen fenced-off pumpjacks were still playing teeter-totter amidst high-end homes sited on a landscape that cunningly disguised its worst ravages. Residents bathing in the prestige of living in *Caldego Canyon Estates, A Premier Raven Brothers Golf Course Community* were apparently able to ignore any sights, sounds or smells that might have reminded them they dwelt in the middle of a working oilfield.

Some months after moving to Oklahoma, hearing that Shorty played a French Foreign Legionnaire in Victor McLaglen's latest hit, *Under Two Flags,* I went to see it in Tulsa, and enjoyed spotting my cousin onscreen, not that he had lines. But I believe that was his last foray into the picture business nor, evidently, did the Lighthorse contract pan out.

Shorty was one of the Depression's more prominent one-week wonders, but when his week was up still had a life to live. The halls of academe closed to him — the coaching profession, too — he signed with a leading promoter for the professional wrestling circuit. Texas Ted did all right, too, fast becoming a "name" wrestler.

A few years later, my wife and I went to see one of his bouts at the Tulsa Coliseum. In fine shape at 203 pounds, Texas Ted looked like a particularly commanding Greek god as he handily pinned "Cowboy" Rick Rains.

Certainly he entertained the crowd. But it was a mob of brawling drunks launching taunts and catcalls through the smoke of a dreary, stinking arena. Altogether it was a sad, somewhat *cheap* spectacle to see Shorty's fleetness, strength, finesse, charm, imagination and star quality come down to play-acting for abusive inebriates, and I couldn't help thinking how much joy the world threw away when it shut down his college football career.

I'd intended surprising him backstage afterwards, but when it was over it seemed better — *kinder*, really — just to go home.

Shorty retired from wrestling to marry an Iowa farm girl, and played several notable years on a semi-pro football team in Des Moines. When he left off that, he became a crane operator, eventually returning to Texas, to Highland Park in Dallas, where he lived in a lovely modern house with his wife and children.

My career prospered, and before too long I was assistant plant manager in Barnsdall, then manager. Meanwhile, I discovered (and my wife played along, bless her) how easy it was to take whatever Oldsmobile I was driving that year and shoot down to Wilbarger County to see how Uncle Jim was getting on.

He got along fine. With immense satisfaction he raised cattle, on a larger scale than he pretended, always leasing more land, buying what he could, and feeding the birds. Behind his house was a lovely lawn surrounded by fruit trees he carefully nurtured, and when he tossed out his handfuls of sunflower and safflower seeds got all the birds he could want: Nuthatches diving in to steal a single one, titmice, chickadees, jays, mourning doves and, with the first and last light of day, cardinals wearing a crimson to seize the heart. Uncle Jim said they made any tree they chose to sit in an apple tree, and that he found it very peaceful.

The last time I saw him was at the 40th Anniversary dinner of the Last Posse Club. My uncles Eustace and Clois founded that select organization, membership limited to those who served in Uncle Jim's posse chasing Frank Holloway or had a family connection to someone who had. Its 50-some members drawn from the cream of the city's commercial class gathered at the Vernon Country Club. Uncle Jim usually avoided their dinners—said he'd dined out on the Oklahoma Yeggman quite long enough—but attended that one as a concession to my visit. He was very old by that time. I had to bend down to hug him tight.

Over shrimp cocktail, two cousins about ten years old came running up to ask, "Uncle Jim, did you ever shoot anybody?"

"*Wa-al*," he drawled, "once shot the heel off a feller's *boot.*"

Disappointed, the kids fled, but eventually, over coffee and apple pie, brought the same question to me. Uncle Jim was speaking of the tragedy of life's teaching you a thing or two but not how to pass it on to anybody else; tragic even when you know *how* you learned what you learned and so *understand* it can't be handed on. Accounted himself blessed just to be able to feed the birds.

His end came not long afterwards, mercifully swift and only possibly ghastly.

In drought the following August, he took his venerable, acid-green Dodge Power Wagon out onto his range to monitor a little grass fire that came sneaking over from a neighbor's. Motor chugging, Uncle Jim sat for a while just watching. Then the wind, as wind will, freshened and turned, the fire flared up and came his way, coming so fast it sucked up the oxygen and stalled his engine. He couldn't start it up again.

One of his ranch hands heard the starter grind and grind, and lit out for him, but it stopped grinding before he got halfway there. Flames surrounded the truck. Most likely at that point Uncle Jim was mercifully unconscious.

www.ingramcontent.com/pod-product-compliance
Lightning Source LLC
Chambersburg PA
CBHW032024120726
47898CB00002BB/659